ASHLEY BRYAN'S

AFRICAN TALES, UH-HUH

ASHLEY BRYAN'S
AFRICAN TALES,
UH-HUH

Retold and Illustrated by Ashley Bryan

Atheneum Books for Young Readers

Atheneum Books for Young Readers
An imprint of Simon & Schuster Children's Publishing Division
1230 Avenue of the Americas
New York, New York 10020

First Edition

Printed in the United States of America

10   9   8   7   6   5   4   3   2   1

Library of Congress Catalog Card Number: 97-77743

ISBN 0-689-82076-3

Contents

THE OX OF THE WONDERFUL HORNS
Ananse the Spider in Search of a Fool 1
Frog and His Two Wives 9
Elephant and Frog Go Courting 13
Tortoise, Hare, and the Sweet Potatoes 20
The Ox of the Wonderful Horns 27

BEAT THE STORY-DRUM, PUM-PUM
Hen and Frog 43
Why Bush Cow and Elephant Are Bad Friends 54
The Husband Who Counted the Spoonfuls 70
Why Frog and Snake Never Play Together 81
How Animals Got Their Tails 93

LION AND THE OSTRICH CHICKS
Lion and the Ostrich Chicks 115
The Son of the Wind 136
Jackal's Favorite Game 152
The Foolish Boy 172

The Ox of the Wonderful Horns and Other African Folktales

Ananse the Spider
in Search of a Fool

W e do not mean, we do not really mean, that what we
are going to say is true.

Hear my account of Spider Ananse and the fish traps.

Spider Ananse once lived by the sea. There were plenty
of fish in those waters. Yes, there were fish to be caught for
those who had traps made and set. But Ananse was not one
to be working like that.

"I'd like to catch and sell fish," he thought, "the regular
type and the shellfish, too. But if I'm to do that, I must hire
a fool to make, set, and pull the traps."

Spider was sure he'd have no trouble finding a fool. Once
he did, he planned to make great catches of fish, which he'd
sell in the market for cash. He would keep all the money
for himself and grow rich in the fish business.

"I'll pay the fool a few regular fish and maybe even some

1

shellfish," he told himself. "But as for money, of course, the fool will get none!"

So Spider Ananse set out to find a fool. He walked about the fishing village, calling, "I want a fool. I want a fool."

He saw a woman cooking. "I am looking for a fool," he said.

"A fool," she said, mocking him and shaking her wooden spoon. Spider ran off to the shore, where on the beach, he saw a busy fisherman.

"I am looking for a fool," said Spider.

"A pool?" asked the fisherman.

"No! A fool," said Spider.

"A tool?" asked the fisherman.

"A fool, a fool," howled Spider as he hurried off. "A fool indeed," he muttered, "but deaf."

And everywhere Ananse looked it was the same. No one listened to him. Nowhere could a fool be found.

After a long time, Ananse met Osana the Hawk. This time Ananse began in a new way. "Come," he said, "let's go and set fish traps."

But Osana had heard that Ananse was hunting a fool to go fishing, so he said, "Oh, I have no need to set fish traps. I have plenty of meat to eat."

Later Ananse met Anene the Crow. "Let us go and set fish traps," Ananse said.

"Why not?" said Crow. "I'll go with you."

"Wait here," said Spider Ananse, almost bursting with joy. "I won't be long." He ran home to get his knife.

While Ananse was gone, Anene the Crow rested in the shade of a silk-cotton tree. And when Hawk was sure that Spider was gone, he flew down.

"Watch out for Ananse," Osana warned. "Don't go with

him on this fish trap-setting trip. He's looking for a fool. He wants someone else to do the work. But he plans to sell all the regular fish, and the shellfish as well, and keep all the cash from the catch for himself."

"*Bakoo!*" said Anene the Crow. "I did not know. But now I do. Thank you Osana. Don't say any more. I will go with Ananse, and we shall see who does the work and who gets the money."

Spider Ananse soon returned with his knife. He and Crow set out at once for the bush to cut palm branches for traps.

When they came to a palm tree, Crow said to Spider, "Ananse, give me the knife. I will go cut the branches. You can sit here and take the weariness of my hard work."

Spider replied, "Anene, do you take me for a fool? No! I will do the cutting. You will sit aside and take the weariness of my work."

So Ananse the Spider did all of the cutting, while Anene the Crow sat aside sighing and yawning in weariness.

When Ananse had finished cutting the palms, Anene helped him tie them into a neat bundle.

Then Crow said, "Ananse, let me carry the bundle. You can trek after me and take the aches and pains of this back-breaking work."

"Oh, no," said Spider. "You must take me for a fool! Here! You help steady the load on my head. I will carry, and you can take the aches."

So Crow followed sighing and yawning and groaning beautifully, every step of the way. And Ananse carried.

When they reached Spider's hut, Crow helped Spider set the load on the ground.

"Now let me make the fish traps," said Crow. "Yes, let

me. I'll show you how. You can take the fatigue of my labors."

Spider replied, "Anene, never! Everyone knows that I'm a great weaver. Leave the trap making to me. You take the fatigue."

Crow chose the most comfortable mat in Spider's hut and stretched out on his back. There he lay, sighing and yawning and groaning and bawling, more woefully than ever.

"Fool," said Spider. "Have you no sense? Just listen to your moaning. It sounds as if you were dying."

Spider Ananse began to spin. He spun and he wove and he made palm mesh for the fish traps. He worked till they were well made and ready to be set.

"Let me carry the fish traps to the water," said Crow. "It's your turn to take the tiredness of all this trap making."

Spider said, "No, no, Anene! None of your tricks. I'll take the traps, and you can take the tiredness of the task."

They set out for the shore. Spider walked carefully, balancing the traps. Crow staggered behind sighing and yawning and groaning and bawling all the way.

At the beach, Crow said, "Father Spider, a beast lives in the sea. Let me stand in the water and set the fish traps. If the beast should bite me, then you can take the death."

Spider said, "Anene, I swear that that is not a bit fair. I shall set the traps. If the beast bites me, then you shall die."

So Spider Ananse toiled in the sea, setting the fish traps. No beast bit. And Anene watched comfortably. Then the two returned to Spider's hut and slept.

The next morning they arose at dawn and hurried down to the sea. They opened the traps and found two fish as their catch.

Crow said, "Ananse, these two fish are for you. Tomorrow, when the traps have caught four, it will be my turn to take them."

Spider exclaimed, "What a cheat you are! Do you take me for a fool? No sir! These two are yours. Tomorrow, I'll take the four."

Anene the Crow took the fish and cooked them. He made a fine dish of fufu and fish and ate it all himself.

The next day Spider and Crow examined the traps and found four fish.

Crow said, "Ananse, these four fish are yours. I'll take the next batch, whatever the catch. With this bait, we're bound to get eight."

Spider said, "I'm no fool! I withdraw my claim to these four. You take these and tomorrow I'll have the eight."

Crow took the fish and fried the four. He made a fine dish of fufu and fried fish and ate it all himself.

The next day when they inspected the traps, Spider counted eight fish as their catch.

"Take them, Ananse," said Crow. "I'll go back to the hut and wait for tomorrow's catch of sixteen."

Spider said, "I am no fool, Anene. You take the eight fish. I'll have tomorrow's sixteen."

Crow took the fish and baked the eight. He made a fine dish of fufu and baked fish and ate it all himself.

The next morning sixteen fish were caught in the traps. And by now the fish traps were well worn out.

Anene the Crow said, "Ananse, these fish traps are rotten. They will not catch fish any longer. But each trap will fetch a price in the marketplace. You take the sixteen fish and give me the rotten fish traps to sell."

"Oh, no!" said Spider. "You take the fish and sell them if

you can. I shall sell the rotten fish traps and keep the cash."

Crow picked up the sixteen fish, and Spider picked up his rotten fish traps. Together they went to the nearby village market.

A crowd soon surrounded Crow. People bargained and bid and bought his fish. In no time at all he had sold the sixteen. If he had had more, he would have sold more. But he did well, just the same, for he had a great mound of gold dust in his feathered purse.

When the crowd broke up, Spider Ananse still sat with his unsold traps.

Crow said to him, "Don't just sit there with your wares. Take up those perfectly rotten fish traps and let people discover that you have them. Walk around and talk about your treasured traps. Cry out! Let the villagers hear your voice. Make a loud noise. Don't think you can sell by sitting in silence."

Crow's fiery speech so inspired Spider that he leaped to his feet, lifted his traps, and sang out in a burst of pride and enthusiasm:

> "Rotten fish traps for sale
> Rare, bedraggled, and old
> Treat your son and yourself
> Pay in cowries or gold."

The village chief was astonished to hear such a ridiculous cry from the market place. Never before had his people been so insulted by a stranger.

"But where does this fellow come from?" he asked. "Send him to me!"

Spider Ananse went quickly at the call, calculating a sale

in cowries and gold. He was still busy making these calculations when the chief thundered:

"Do you suppose this is a village of fools?"

Spider trembled.

"Your friend Crow came and sold fine fish for a good profit. Did you sit by and not take notice? Then why do you seek to dispose of your useless, rotten fish traps among us?"

The chief was so angry that he called his men and said, "Flog him!"

Spider Ananse tried to flee, but he tripped over the loose palm strips of his rotten fish traps. As he flailed about to free himself, he became more entangled in the mesh until he was caught like a fish in his own fish traps.

As the blows drummed on Spider's back, he cried, *"Pui-pui, pui-pui!* Why do they beat p-po-poor me?"

Tears of pain flowed from Ananse's eyes. Then suddenly they became tears of shame. For, at last, Spider Ananse realized that when one seeks to make a fool of another, he is bound to make a bigger fool of himself.

This is my story. Whether it be bitter or whether it be sweet, take some of it elsewhere and let the rest come back to me.

Frog and His Two Wives

Listen, let me tell the story of Frog Kumbuto who married two wives.

"*Kuo-kua*," he sang for one wife.

"*Kua-kuo*," he sang for the other.

He sprang high into the air. *Whish!* Twirling both legs, he whirled himself about and came down. *Whump!* He jumped again into the skies. *Whee!* It was a wonder to have two wives.

Frog Kumbuto built each wife a good house of her own on his land.

The first wife chose the sycamore grove on the east of his land. There he built her house. *Bam!*

The second wife chose the palm grove on the west of Frog's land. There he built her house. *Bohm!*

The middle ground was where Frog liked to be. Berry

bushes grew there with berries that Frog liked to lick, nibble, and bite for breakfast. And there was, as well, a tall nut tree for noonday shade and nuts; and nearby there lay a small rush marsh for an evening splash and bath. It was in the middle that Frog built his house. *Bosh!*

Well, the first wife cooked one meal for Frog each day. And the second wife cooked the other meal. The east house wife cooked for Frog as the sun rose in the east. The west house wife cooked for Frog as the sun set in the west. It was a fine plan. Frog swelled with pride when he saw how well it worked.

The sun shone day after day. And day after day for many months Frog ate at morning in the east and at evening in the west. But then the rainy season began.

Frog Kumbuto loved the rain. He sauntered about in delight. But by the thirteenth day of the rainy spell, Frog's two wives had become confused about the time of day. So it happened that one gray day, without knowing whether they were coming or going, the wives mixed up the meal-time plan. Well! Both began to cook for Frog at the same time.

Each wife fanned her fire and stirred her pot. Frog Kumbuto, not thinking about it, lay on his rush mat and smelled the delicious odor of juicy mush from the east and the aroma of lush spicy mush from the west. *Haah!*

In time the mush was cooked. Both wives looked up to see if Frog was coming. But Frog had not moved. What!

The first wife called her little son and said, "Hop now and fetch your father!"

The second wife said to her small daughter, "Rush now and fetch your father!"

Both children left quickly to fetch Father Frog. Skip-

ping and jumping and hopping from east and from west, they arrived at the same spot at the same time. *Thump!* They fell down on the rush mat beside Frog Kumbuto.

Regaining their feet and their breath, each child pulled one of Frog's arms as they sang out together, "Father come with me! Come with me! It's time to eat."

Now Frog was in a fix. He was pulled to the east. He was pulled to the west. Woe! He freed his arms and beat his breast.

"Oh, no!" he groaned as he spun around. He clutched his stomach. He pounded the ground.

"Both wives are calling, 'Come! Come! Come!' They are two, and I am one. If I go east to eat first, the west wife will pester me. 'Aha,' she'll say, 'so east wife is your chief wife, eh?' If I decide to feast with the west wife first, then the east wife will cry, 'Aho, Kumbuto! From the start I thought the west wife was your best beloved!'"

Frog sat down and wailed. He was so upset that he garbled his words. His cracked bass voice called out:

"Rye bam in bubble! I tam tin tubble!" Till finally he croaked it right: "I am in trouble!"

Now friends, the story is as I have told it. Plucky Frog Kumbuto married two wives. All went well until the day that both called him to mush at once. To this day he does not know what to do.

He sits in the marsh and cries:

"Kuo-kua! Kua-Kuo!"

It sounds funny, I know. Some people joke and say:

"Listen, Frog is croaking!"

But no! Frog is speaking. He is saying:

"I am in trouble!"

Pity poor Frog.

Elephant and Frog Go Courting

I never tire of telling the tale of Mr. Elephant and Mr. Frog who were courting the girls at the same house.

Frog and Elephant were enormously popular with the girls at that house. They were thoughtful and generous and always brought presents of flowers or fruit when they visited.

Indeed, everyone who knew Elephant and Frog agreed that, despite obvious differences, the two had much in common.

They were both very handsome, each in his own way, of course. They both loved the water, and both relished a walk through the forest, especially when the path led to the pretty girls' house. And although they were not the same size, they were the same age.

But why go on listing ways in which Frog and Elephant

were alike? There are so many and that's hardly the story. So let's go on.

It happened that one afternoon Frog visited the girls alone. He sat with them near the house in the shade of a silk-cotton tree, and they all sipped cool coconut milk.

The girls surrounded Frog and laughed at his witty talk. His conversation was more charming and clever than ever. He felt he was king of the forest! So when Elephant's sweetheart began to speak with great eloquence of Elephant's grace and elegance, at once Frog became angry.

He puffed himself up as large as he dared. He swelled with importance and said to her, "You know, of course, that Mr. Elephant is my horse."

"Is that true? Is that true?" the girls chorused. They were so excited that they danced around Frog. Well, now, Frog felt big, bigger even than Mr. Elephant. And when he left he hopped off into the forest as if he owned it all.

Elephant came to visit that night. As they saw him coming through the forest, the girls said to his sweetheart, "Look! Here comes Mr. Frog's horse!"

Elephant's sweetheart ran out to meet him. He gave her a basket of wild cherries, a bouquet of wild flowers, a tame hug, and a shy kiss.

The girl, however, hardly thanked Elephant at all for this. She was so full of Frog's remark that she simply blurted out, "We heard today from Mr. Frog that you are his horse."

"Better that than the other way round," quipped Elephant, and he laughed uproariously. The girls laughed, too, but then they repeated what Frog had said. They obviously believed it.

"Now wait a m-minute," stammered Elephant. "Me?

M-m-me? Mr. Frog's horse?"

"That's what he said."

"Ridiculous! He was k-k-kidding of course!"

"Oh, no," said Elephant's sweetheart. "He swore to us that he was serious."

Elephant was furious. He fumed and trumpeted and left in a rage. Behind him, he could hear the girls laughing as he went. He felt small, even smaller than Mr. Frog.

The next day Elephant went in search of Frog. He looked everywhere and finally caught him frisking in the river.

"Hello, Grandfather," Frog called affectionately. "Want to race?"

Elephant could not bring himself to say so much as one word. He simply reached out with his trunk and snatched Mr. Frog out of the water. He set his startled friend down *plop!* on a grass patch.

"Now look here, Grandson," he said still shaking with anger but at least not stammering. "Did you tell the girls that I was your horse?"

"What's that?" croaked Frog hopping up and down. "What? What? Easy there, Grandfather." Frog balled up his fists and advanced on Elephant menacingly. "Nobody accuses me of anything like that!"

"Calm down, Grandson," said Elephant backing away. He was impressed by Frog's display of anger and innocence. "It was my sweetheart. She said you swore I was your horse!"

"Now that's crazy!" Frog spluttered. "Come along, Grandfather! We'll find those girls and settle this foolishness right this minute."

Frog started out ahead of Elephant, but he soon fell far behind. Elephant was anxious to reach the girls, but he wanted to arrive with Frog. So he sat and waited. "Hurry up, Grandson," he called.

Frog caught up at last, huffing and puffing, and limping besides. "Oh, oh what a trail!" he whined. "I must have stepped on a thorn. My poor foot's sore. I can't keep up with you at all. I'll have to go home and tend to my foot."

"What?" trumpeted Elephant. "You can't turn back now, Grandson! Listen, the girls will take care of your foot once we get that remark settled. Hop up on my back. That way we'll arrive together. It won't take long."

"Thanks, Grandfather, but I really don't want to be a burden!"

"Oh, be quiet, Grandson! Don't be silly!"

So Frog hopped up on Elephant's back.

Elephant's back was broad, and the ride was smooth. Nevertheless Frog flopped about, flailing hands and feet as if he were about to fall off.

"Grandfather! Grandfather!" he soon shouted into Elephant's ear. "I'll have more than a hurt foot by the time we arrive if I don't get some reins to steady myself up here!"

Elephant stopped and stooped, and Frog limped off. Elephant wanted Frog to be quick about getting the reins, so he helped Frog pull long tendrills from a tall banyan tree.

Frog plaited the tendrils into a strong string, which he bound across Elephant's mouth. Then he limped back into place.

"Well, Grandfather! What a difference!" Frog exclaimed as he directed Elephant with the reins.

They went on steadily.

Suddenly Frog started whirling his arms as if he'd lost his mind. "My word, Grandfather!" he shouted. "We must have hit a cloud of flies and mosquitoes! I haven't seen this

many in all my born days. Do stop! I'd better get me a green-twig switch to flick off these rascal insects. Otherwise we'll be eaten alive before we arrive!"

Once more Elephant stopped and stooped. Frog limped down and moved slowly to a bush. He broke off a neat twig switch and twirled it gently as he returned to his place on Elephant's back.

Frog swished the twig-whip in great arcs and held the reins slack until they reached the edge of the forest. Just ahead, by the silk-cotton tree, was the house of the girls.

"Quick, Grandson," Elephant called. "Hop down. We are almost there."

Frog pretended not to hear. Instead he tightened the reins, pinching the tenderest tissues of Elephant's mouth. Elephant reared up in pain then plunged ahead. But Frog held on.

The girls heard the commotion and came to their door just as Elephant, with Frog astride, went racing by. Frog

17

was holding the reins smartly with one hand and whirling the twig whip with the other.

When they were well past the house, Frog jerked the left rein sharply and Elephant spun around. As they galloped back, the girls applauded. Really, they had never seen a more dramatic display of horsemanship.

Elephant sped with Frog into the forest along the same path they had come from in the first place. As soon as Frog knew the girls could no longer see them, he let go of the reins and flipped himself into the overhanging branches of the tree.

"Thanks for the ride, Grandfather horse," Frog croaked. And he hopped off quickly until he was lost among the leaves.

Elephant buffeted and butted and battered the trees. Bananas fell. Coconuts fell. Mangoes and figs fell. But no Frog fell.

Finally Elephant gave up. All the way home the birds sang, but that did not cheer him up at all. For in his mind he could only hear the girls saying, "So it's true. It's true indeed. Mr. Elephant is the horse of Mr. Frog."

There! I have told my tale of Elephant and Frog. Whether good, whether bad, there is nothing to add. I have finished.

Tortoise, Hare, and the Sweet Potatoes

Listen, brothers and sisters, to this story of how Tortoise outwitted Hare.

Hare was a born trickster. He was always dreaming up new riddles and tricks to try on others. He'd spring an impossible riddle, wait a little, then rattle off the answer. Riddles and tricks, Hare never tired of either.

Tortoise on the other hand was much too busy keeping her little pond clean to worry about tricking anyone. Animals came from field and forest, far and near, to drink in the pond where she lived.

Tortoise believed in the proverb, "Give the passing traveller water and you will drink news yourself." So, although she rarely left her pool, her visitors kept her well informed. She knew more than most and was seldom fooled.

It happened one season then that the news Tortoise

heard again and again was disgracefully bad. Someone was stealing, stealing food from all the fields around. Now most creatures were willing to give when another was hungry. But stealing was taboo.

Everyone asked, "Who would do what's taboo?" And no one knew. But Tortoise had a few well-founded ideas.

One day Hare came by Tortoise's pond. He drank his fill, then was ready for mischief. "Aha! Now to muddy the pond and have a little fun," he thought. He had never cared for the proverb, "Do not fill up the well after having drunk. Where would you drink tomorrow?"

Tortoise was on her guard, however, and all Hare could do was sit beside her and ask riddles. Tortoise answered every one.

"I know one you can't answer," said Hare. "Tell me the thing that you can beat without leaving a scar?"

"I live by it and I drink it," said Tortoise. "Water."

So Hare gave up trying to catch Tortoise with riddles. But he was not through.

After a while he said, "Now old Tortoise, let's go and till a field together."

"Me! Till the land? I can just manage to scratch out my little garden patch. How could I hoe a whole field with my short legs?"

"Short legs? Your legs are beautiful. Just the right length for hoeing."

"Do say! But how could I hold a hoe?"

"No problem at all. I'll tie you to it. I'd love to do that for you."

There was truth in that statement, Tortoise decided. Hare knew how to trick people, all right. But she wasn't taken in. She said aloud, "I don't think I'll try, thanks."

21

So they sat in silence. And after a while Hare said, "I'm hungry, Sis. Aren't you?"

"A little, but I don't have a leaf left in my garden."

"Well, poor thing, let me help you. I came upon a wide field of good things on my way here. Come on! Let's help ourselves to some of Wild Boar's sweet potatoes."

"Ooo, ooo! What are you saying? You know better than that, Mr. Hare. No pilfering!"

So they sat on in silence, Hare not willing to give up.

And after a while Tortoise became really hungry. Besides she had a few worthwhile ideas.

"Where did you say that field of sweet potatoes was?" she asked.

"It's not far, just past the bush."

"Well now, said Tortoise, seeming to overcome her scruples, "I guess Wild Boar won't miss a few."

Off they went together. And when they came to Wild Boar's field it was no job at all to root out the sweet potatoes. Soon Hare's sack was filled.

Hare with a great show of strength steadied the bag on Tortoise's back, and they headed for the bush to cook the potatoes. When they found a good quiet spot, they gathered dry grass and made a crackling fire in which the sweet potatoes were soon roasted.

"Mmm-yum," said Tortoise as she bit into one.

"Wait a minute," said Hare. "Did you hear that?"

"Mmm-yum," said Tortoise, her mouth full of sweet potato.

"Stop munching and mumbling!" said Hare. "What if we're caught?"

"Mmm-um-yum," said Tortoise, reaching for another sweet potato.

"Wow-wow," said Hare, "do you want to be beaten and bitten by Wild Boar? Put down that potato! We've got to scout around first and make sure that Boar's not after us."

Hare forced Tortoise to stop eating, and they went off in opposite directions to scout the field.

Tortoise who had a good notion of what was afoot and was ready, waddled a few reluctant steps; Hare bounded out of sight. As soon as he was gone, Tortoise turned back, took another sweet potato, and crawled into the empty sack.

"Mmm-yum," she said. She was about to crawl out for another when suddenly a rain of roasted sweet potatoes fell around her. Hare was back, very quietly, very quickly.

"Good," said Tortoise, biting into another sweet potato, "saves me the trouble."

Old trickster Hare filled his sack in a hurry.

"Mistress Tortoise," he shouted then. "Get going! Take off! Run for your life! Wild Boar and his big, fat wife are coming."

He threw the bag over his back. "Save yourself! Fly!" he cried, but inside he thought: "Best trick in ages. Now to put some miles between me and Slowpoke." He took off, running and laughing as hard as he could.

Tortoise made herself comfortable in the sack. She ate one sweet potato after another. "Too bad Hare is missing the feast," she thought. "But maybe he prefers running to eating."

Hare ran as fast and as far as he could. By the time he stopped to rest, Tortoise had eaten all of the finest and fatest sweet potatoes. In fact, there was only one very small sweet potato left.

"Aha good," said Hare as he put his hand into the sack. "Too bad Tortoise is miles away."

"Sweet potatoes," Hare sang, "sweet, sw-eeeet potatoes!" Tortoise put the last sweet potato into Hare's outstretched hand.

When Hare saw the size of it, he cried, "Ha! What a miserable one this is. I didn't run my head off for that!" And he flung it into the bushes.

Hare put his hand back into the sack. This time he felt a big one, a nice firm, juicy one.

"Oho!" he chortled, "here's a beauty. What a prize!"

Imagine Hare's surprise when he saw what he had in his hand.

"Mistress Tortoise!" he cried as he dropped her to the ground.

Hare shook out the sack. Tears of unbelief welled up in his eyes when he saw it was empty. "My potatoes, the sweet ones I rooted up . . . oh no, oh no! You didn't eat mine, too? Sister Tortoise, how could you be so unfair?"

But Mistress Tortoise didn't stand around for the lecture. She took to her toes and scuttled away to her pond as fast as she could go.

Hungry Hare lay on the ground and screeched, "Woe, woe, that wily Mistress Tortoise ate all my sweet potatoes. Wa, Waa. How awful of her. When I think that I carried her all the while, I could cry!"

And that's just what he did.

The Ox of the Wonderful Horns

There are those who enjoy telling of the boy who made his fortune with nothing but a pair of ox horns.

Mungalo, that was the boy's name, and he was the son of a wealthy chief. His father had many wives. They loved their husband, but they were jealous of Mungalo's mother. She was the first and favorite wife. They dared not offend her, but they found ways to worry Mungalo. They found ways to be cruel to him.

But each day when Mungalo went out with the sheep and the goats, he tapped the sparrow drum he always took with him. The sound of the little drum made him forget how badly he was treated by his father's wives.

Each wife did her best to outshout the rest when Mungalo returned in the evening with the animals. Just as his head cleared the crest of the hill near the kraal, he'd hear their calls:

"Mungalo! Mungalo! Mungalo!"

Each wife always had a job for him to do—at once! Mungalo did all he could as fast as he could, but nothing ever pleased his hard-hearted mothers.

It was as the proverb says: "They gave him a basket to carry water."

Only his own mother was loving and gave him toys and kindness and words of comfort. But, alas, Mungalo was still a child when she died. The toys she had given him, especially some little clay oxen that she had made, broke one by one, until he had none left. But he kept whole in his heart his mother's promise that when he was old enough his father would give him a great white ox.

The years passed. Each day at dawn Mungalo set out to find a good grazing place for the sheep and the goats. While he worked, his brothers, the sons of many mothers, played. When he came home, he found no welcome but more work. Yet Mungalo suffered his mistreatment in silence and said nothing to his father.

After his initiation into the tribe, Munaglo's father gave him a great white ox, just as his mother had promised. It was a beautiful beast with wonderful horns, the finest of all of his father's cattle.

Mungalo thought that then he would be treated with respect. He was old enough to herd the great oxen, and he owned the most admired ox of all.

But the jealousy of his mean mothers only inspired them to find more ways of making Mungalo unhappy. So he decided he must leave home.

One morning, he mounted the great white ox and journeyed until he had left the land of his father far behind.

For seven days and seven nights the boy and the ox

travelled on. They stopped only to rest and to eat the food of the lands they traversed.

Toward noon on the eighth day, they crossed a wide plain. It was so hot that shimmering heat waves made the ground seem to heave and swell like an ocean.

Mungalo was hungry and thirsty. He looked about him. But nowhere on that dry plain did he see the least sign of plant or tree or water.

Mungalo stroked the ox gently and said, "Dear friend, I've led you from a land we knew to an unknown plain. I had hoped to escape the curse of my father's wives. But what could be worse than to die here of hunger and thirst?"

Moved by his friend's distress, the ox spoke:

"Mungalo, listen! At your command
Food or clothes or house and land
I can provide. Strike my horns.
Three times the right, you'll have your wish
Twice the left and all will vanish."

Mungalo did as the ox bid. He struck the right horn three times. Suddenly cool grass covered the ground. On it were bowls of pungent food and luscious fruit.

Mungalo leaped from the ox's back and thanked his friend. Together they ate and drank and were refreshed.

Then Mungalo mounted the ox and struck the left horn twice. Immediately the remaining food was gone. It seemed to have vanished into the horn itself.

The two travelled on.

For seven days and seven nights Mungalo and the ox of the wonderful horns crossed the open plains. They stopped only to rest, to sleep, and to refresh themselves with the food struck from the horns of the great white ox.

At last they came to a virgin forest. Great trees and roots and vines like tangled ropes barred the way. But, at the touch of the ox's hooves, roots and vines moved aside. Tall ferns parted. Low leaves and branches lifted above Mungalo's head. The movement of the plants allowed thin beams of light to come in, and sun spots scattered and danced like balls of gold. The whole scene seemed enchanted to Mungalo.

Deep in the forest their path opened upon a clearing. There a herd of cattle grazed. At the head of the group stood a large bull.

Mungalo saw no way around the herd, and the leader challenged the route the white ox took. The bull tossed his head and pawed the ground as the travellers approached. The earth shook, and Mungalo trembled; but the ox spoke:

> "Do not fear the might
> Of this fierce bull. We'll fight,
> And I will win. We've far

To go until we are
Before the towering mountain wall
Where I will fight. Where I will fall."

During the battle Mungalo crouched at one edge of the clearing. The cattle lined the other side.

In the force and fury of the fight, torn grass rose from the ground and formed a dark green cloud around the ox and the bull. The sound of clashing horns and striking hooves drummed like a huge sparrow drum. The noise filled the clearing.

When the tumult stilled, the grass cloud settled and Mungalo saw the fierce bull dead. His ox of the wonderful horns came toward him.

Mungalo leaped lightly astride the ox and the herd parted. The two passed unharmed through the strange creatures and into the forest.

Seven days and seven nights Mungalo and the great white ox pushed on. They journeyed through dense jungles and deep ravines. They crossed hills and wide streams.

Finally they crossed a narrow stream and came upon carefully planted, fertile fields. It seemed strange to Mungalo that no one was laboring or gathering there.

Then he saw, looming ahead, a towering mountain. It rose like a huge wall. But some great force had, it seemed once moved the land beneath the mountain and had split the high stone wall. So now a narrow cleft led through the mountain to a village beyond.

Guarding the narrow pass was a huge bull, looking more fierce than the last beast the ox had battled. Nearby grazed a dun-colored herd of cattle.

Mungalo immediately recognized the place as the one

described by the ox. In sorrow he fell forward and lay still on the ox's back. Then, for some reason strengthened, he slid down, touched the wonderful horns, and rubbed the dear beast's forehead.

The ox spoke:

> *"Goodbye Mungalo. At your command*
> *Food or clothes or house and land*
> *My horns will give. When I am gone*
> *This power remains for you alone."*

In the battle that followed, Mungalo's ox of the wonderful horns was killed. When the dust cloud the fight had stirred up settled, the ox lay on the ground, and the bull and its herd had disappeared.

Mungalo severed the horns from the ox's head and bound them carefully to the belt at his waist. Tears filled his eyes. When they cleared, the ox had disappeared as completely as the bull and the cows.

Mungalo walked slowly through the cleft in the mountain and came out at the village beyond. There he saw the townspeople cooking a tough root. Mungalo soon learned that this weed was the only food left in the village. The mysterious herd had pounded through the village days before and had scattered the grain that had been stored.

When the villagers saw the direction from which Mungalo had come, they asked in surprise, "How did you get through the pass? A huge fierce bull has blocked the path for days."

Mungalo did not wish to tell the tale of the great white ox. He did not want anyone to know the secret of the magic horns, so he said, "No herd or huge fierce bull was there

when I went through. You are fools to feed upon roots when your fields are full of food."

The villagers rejoiced when they heard that the mountain pass was clear. Drumming began, and the people danced. The chief singer sang praise songs to the stranger for his good news. Now the people could return to their fields without fear.

The singer invited Mungalo into his hut for the night. Since they were both hungry, Mungalo secretly tapped the right horn. Three times he tapped it and food appeared before them.

The singer was astonished to see a sudden abundance of food before him. He ate heartily, determined all the while to learn the trick. He smiled and quickly poured more palm wine each time Mungalo emptied his gourd. But Mungalo's tongue did not trip and tell the secret.

At the end of the feast Mungalo tapped the left horn

twice, and the food was gone. Both men settled down to sleep.

But during the night the singer, who had only pretended to sleep, crept to Mungalo's side. He had guessed the secret, and now he untied the magic horns from Mungalo's belt, replacing them with two others. He hid the wonderful horns and lay down again.

In the morning the whole village rose early to go through the mountain pass to their fields. Mungalo thanked his host and started on his way. He was happy for he knew that his friend's spirit lived with him in the wonderful horns, and he sang as he went along.

Near noon the sun shone from straight overhead and Mungalo's shadow hid underfoot. He was hungry and tired, so he stopped to rest.

The first thing he did was to strike the right horn three times, but nothing happened. He tried again, but no food came from the horn. Then Mungalo knew that his wonderful horns had been exchanged for worthless ones.

There was nothing to do but go straight back to the hut in the village where he had spent the night. Once there, he heard the singer chanting praise songs as he tapped the horns. But no matter how exalted his praises to the color and curve of the horns, and no matter how skillfully he rapped them, nothing happened.

Finally, in a fury, he flung the horns into a far corner of the hut. In his rage, he rammed his head against the door so hard he burst through.

The villagers could not understand why the singer was so wild. They knew nothing of the magic horns. And now that they had returned from their fields, they were too busy cooking and eating their own good food to care.

Mungalo entered the hut, took the magic horns, and left the others. He knew now that the good of the wonderful horns could not fall into the hands of a thief. And he was glad.

As he travelled on, Mungalo sensed the spirit and power of the ox protecting him all along the way. He did not count how many times the sun rose and set upon his adventures. Each day he walked contented, seeing and hearing strange and wonderful things. Each night he slept beneath the stars believing that the ox's horns kept him from harm.

Mungalo paid little attention to himself. He was too busy marvelling at the wonders about him. He never never saw that his clothes were spotted and torn. He did not know that he was streaked with the dust of travel. Yet he longed now and then for a companion. So one night when he saw a house by a field, he decided to stop. He knocked at the door, and a man came.

The man looked at Mungalo, turned, and closed the door. He did not invite Mungalo in.

Mungalo could not understand this until the next day when he came to a stream and looked at himself in the still water. He scarcely recognized his own reflection. He laughed remembering the look on the man's face. No wonder he had been turned away!

Mungalo splashed and washed and swam until he was clean. Then he dried in the sun and wished for new clothes. He struck the horn as he spoke:

"I knocked at a door
I was chased as a thief.
Please dress me in clothes
Due the son of a chief."

Immediately an array of marvellous clothes and ornaments was displayed on the branches of low bushes. Mungalo dressed in the bright cloths he liked best. He chose well-wrought spiral silver pendants, bead ornaments and gold rings. He refastened his belt of horns and draped a gorgeous mantle over his shoulders. Then he entered the next village.

Here, Mungalo's royal appearance won for him a warm welcome. He was greeted by the chief of the village and invited to stay in his house. He was treated like a prince, and was served with grace and dignity by the chief's daughter.

The young girl's beauty filled Mungalo's eyes and heart. He gave rich cloths as gifts to the father, and he offered the daughter gold ornaments that glowed against her dark skin.

Three moons passed, and Mungalo shared more and

more in the life of the village. He helped the chief in his duties, and at night the villagers crowded around the fire to hear Mungalo tell tales from the land of his father.

Mungalo's love for the chief's daughter grew, and his acts of generosity and manliness soon won her heart.

After a time they were married. The food furnished by Mungalo's new family and the fine fare from the magic horns provided a feast that lasted for days. The drumming and dancing and singing did not stop until the last of the food had been eaten and the last pot of palm wine had been emptied.

A year later Mungalo returned with his wife to his father's village. The chief's wives prepared a lavish dinner to celebrate the son's return. They saw that their old evil ways had come to no good end. So they forgot their old jealousies and treated him well. They outdid each other in praise for Mungalo, his wife, and his wealth.

Mungalo and his wife settled on the ancestral lands

given him by his father. He wished on the magic horns for a house fit for the son of a chief. Later, as the family grew, he enlarged his fine dwelling by new wishes on the horns.

Mungalo told many tales of his adventures, but he never told the secret of the wonderful horns. Awake they were with him. Asleep they were nearby.

So the spirit of the great white ox stayed close to Mungalo throughout his life. For even when he became the honored leader of the tribe it was said that he was never parted from those wonderful horns.

Beat the
Story-Drum,
Pum-Pum

Hen and Frog

I'VE TOLD ONE TALE, HERE'S ANOTHER
CALL YOUR SISTER, CALL YOUR BROTHER.

FROG AND HEN once met. They walked along together.
   Hen strut two steps, pecked at a bug.
Frog bopped three hops, flicked his tongue at a fly.
Strut two steps, peck at a bug.
Bop three hops, flick at a fly.
Hen flapped her wings and spun around. Frog slapped his
legs and tapped the ground.
   "All in together now," clucked Hen.
   "How do you like the weather now?" croaked Frog.

"O click clack," clucked Hen. "See that dark cloud? That's a sign, I know it. A storm's coming."

Strut two steps, peck at a bug.

"It's still a way far off," said Frog.

Bop three hops, flick at a fly.

"Good!" said Hen. "Then there's time. Frog, let's make a hut before the storm hits."

"A hut? Not me!" said Frog. "Here's a neat hole. I'm going to get into that. Uh-uh, I won't help you make a hut."

"Suit yourself," said Hen. "If you won't help me, then I'll make the hut myself."

Hen set to work and Frog jumped into the hole. While Hen worked, Frog sang:

"Kwee kwo kwa
Kwa kwo kwee
A hole in the ground
Is a hut to me."

Hen was a skillful hut builder. She flipped and she flapped, pieced, pecked and pulled every branch and straw into place. She put in two windows, a door, and thatched the roof, leaving a space in the middle for the smoke of the fireplace.

"Click, clack, cluck," she sang. "Click, clack, cluck, claa, clee."

The dark cloud came closer.

"Quick Frog," said Hen, "there's still time. Help me make a bed for the hut."

Frog sang:
"Kwee kwo kwa
  Kwa kwo kwee
  The ground in the hole
  Is a bed to me."

"Well!" said Hen. "If you won't help me then I'll make the bed myself."

So Hen built the bed all by herself. She lay down to test it.

"O click clack cluck," she sang, "click, clack, cluck, claa, clee."

The dark cloud came even closer.

"Frog," said Hen, "there's still a little time left before the storm hits. Help me gather corn."

Frog sang:

"Kwee kwo kwa
  kwa kwo kwee
  The bugs in the hole
  Are food to me."

"Uh-uh," said Hen. "If you won't help me, then I'll gather the corn myself."

So Hen gathered the corn all by herself. She piled it by the fireplace and then rolled some pumpkins onto the thatched roof. She ran into her hut and latched the door just as the storm broke.

"*Blam-bam-pa-lam! Blam-bam-pa-lam!*"

The thunder rolled, the earth shook, tree branches tossed, and Frog was jostled in his hole.

"Kwa kwee," he sang, "kwee kwaaa!"

The rain came down, it really poured. Hen went to the window and looked out. Frog was standing up in his hole, swaying and singing a riddle song:

"Her children dance madly
  Mama never dances
  Riddle me this, riddle me that,
  Riddle me 'round the answers.
  Mama is a tree trunk
  Her children are the branches."

"Fool," said Hen. "This is no time for riddles."

Frog stamped as he sang. Suddenly, *splish-splash*, what! Water rose in the hole.

"Eh, eh!" cried Frog. "What's happening?"

Slish-slosh, the water rose higher and higher, and Frog was flooded out of his home. He waved to Hen as he floated by her hut, and sang:

"All in together now
  How do you like the weather now?"

"Sing it!" said Hen. "But you'll soon croon another tune."

It wasn't long before the steady force of the rain stung Frog's tender skin, and he began to wail:

"Kwo kwa kwee
  Kwa kwee kwo
  The stinging rain is riddling me
  Where shall I go?"

Frog knew where he planned to go. He bounded for shelter. Hop, hop, hop, hop, hop, hop right up to Hen's hut.

"Hen, Hen!" he cried as he rapped on her door. "May I come into your hut?"

"No," said Hen. "Uh-uh! When I asked you to help me make a hut, you refused."

"If you don't let me come in," said Frog "I'll call Cat, the cat that eats little chickens."

"Go back to your hole!" said Hen.

"Cat! Cat!" yelled Frog. "Come and eat Hen."

"Shh" said Hen. She opened the door. "Hush your mouth! Shame on you, scamp! Come on in."

Frog hopped in and sat by the door. The rain beat down, but

Hen's hut was tight and the rain couldn't get in. Frog leaned against the door drumming his numb toes and rubbing his stinging skin. Hen sat by the fire.

"Hen" said Frog, "may I warm myself by the fire?"

"No," said Hen. "Uh-uh!
  You didn't help me make the hut,
  Hands on your hips.
  You didn't help me gather wood,
  Pursed your lips."

"If you don't let me sit by the fire," said Frog, "I'll call Cat, the cat that eats little chickens."

"That's not fair Frog, you wouldn't dare."

Frog opened the door and cried:

"Cat! Cat! Here's Hen Chick
  Come and eat her! Quick, come quick!"

Hen slammed and bolted the door.

"Scamp!" she said. "You scim-scam-scamp! Go ahead then, sit by the fire."

Frog hopped beside Hen and warmed himself by the fire.

"Umm-umm," he said, "fire sure feels good."

Frog spread his tingling toes to the heat and stroked his skin. Hen busied herself roasting corn. Then she began to eat.

"Hen," said Frog, "may I have some corn?"

"No," said Hen. "Uh-uh!
  You didn't help me make the hut,
  Hands on your hips.
  You didn't help me gather wood,
  Pursed your lips.
  You didn't help me pick the corn,
  Rolled your eyes."

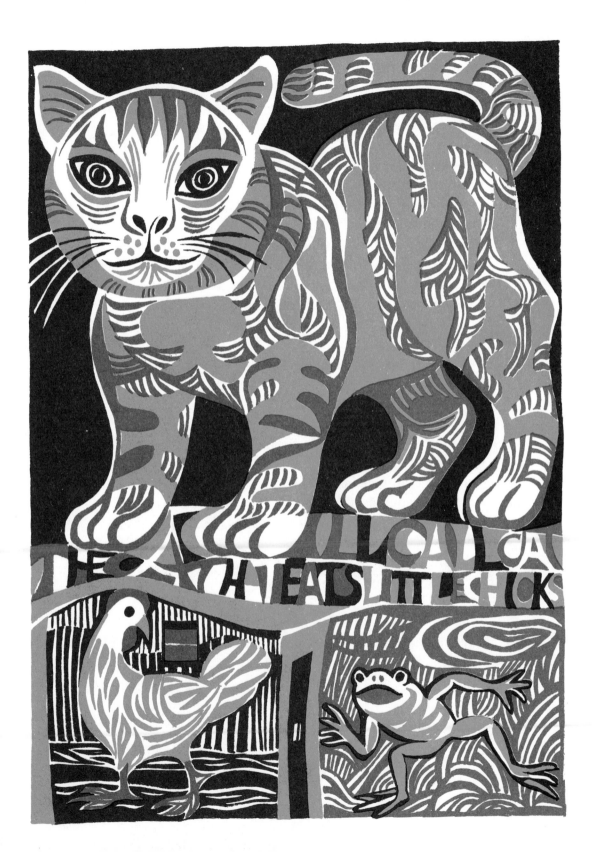

THE CAT CAT CAT
THE CAT EATS LITTLE CHICKS

"Ah! so what," said Frog. "If you don't give me some corn to eat, then I'll call Cat, the cat that eats little chickens."

"And I'll call your bluff," said Hen.

Frog opened the window and called:

"Cat! Cat! Here's Hen Chick

  Come and eat her! Quick, come quick!"

Hen slammed and latched the window.

"Scamp!" she cried. "Greedy scamp! Here, help yourself."

Frog helped himself until all the corn was eaten. Then he rubbed his stomach, stretched himself and leaned back on his elbow. The food and the fire made Frog drowsy. He yawned.

"Hen," said Frog, "may I lie on your bed?"

"No!" said Hen. "Uh-uh!"

  You didn't help me make the hut,

  Hands on your hips.

  You didn't help me gather wood,

  Pursed your lips.

  You didn't help me pick the corn,

  Rolled your eyes.

  You didn't help me make the bed,

  An' it ain't your size!"

"If you don't let me lie on your bed," said Frog, "I'll call Cat, the cat that eats little chickens."

"Shh, shh!" said Hen.

Frog jumped up and down and bawled:

"Cat! Cat Here's Hen Chick

  Come and eat her! Quick, come quick!"

"Quiet, scamp!" said Hen "Lazy scamp! Go ahead then, lie on my bed."

Frog lay on Hen's bed and fell fast asleep. He was still snoring loudly when the rain stopped.

Hen stepped outdoors to see if the pumpkins were still on the roof. She kept an eye cocked for Cat.

"Well, all right!" she said. "Just where I left them."

She went in and slammed the door, *bligh!*

Frog sprang awake. The noise frightened him, and he dived under the bed.

"Come on out Frog," said Hen. "The storm's over."

Frog crawled out.

"I'm hungry," he said.

"Climb onto the roof and fetch us some pumpkins," said Hen. "I'll cook, and we'll eat."

"Umm," said Frog. "Umm, pumpkin. I love pumpkin." But he still just sat on the edge of the bed.

Hen looked out of the window. She saw a small dark cloud
in the distance. She knew that sign well, uh-huh!

"Hop to it, Frog," she said. "You can rest while I'm cooking
a pumpkin."

Frog went outside and climbed up onto the roof. He dis-
lodged a pumpkin from the thatch and rolled it down. Hen
stood by the window and watched the dark cloud approach. It
came faster and faster and grew bigger and bigger and . . .

It was Hawk!

Hawk spied Frog rolling the pumpkins off the roof. Frog was too busy to notice anything, not even Hawk's shadow as Hawk hovered over the thatch.

Hawk closed his wings and fell swiftly, silently. Suddenly, *flump!* Hawk snatched Frog in his claws and took off.

"Help! Help!" cried Frog. "Hen help me, help! I'm being carried off."

"Eh, eh!" said Hen. "Why don't you call Cat? You know, the Cat that eats little chickens. Eh? Click, clack, cluck, claa, clee."

Hen watched the scene safely from her window. Hawk soared upwards.

"Good!" said Hen. "That's it. Take the little so-and-so away. I've had more than enough of him, little tough buttocks!"

Hawk flew higher and higher. If Frog did call Cat, Cat did not come.

So that was that. Hawk took Frog away, and Hen could relax again. She cooked the pumpkin and sat down to eat. She was so happy that she ate eighteen plates of pumpkin without a stop. Then she lay back on her little bed and sang:

"Click clack cluck
Click claa clee.
I ate pumpkin,
Pumpkin didn't eat me."

Why Bush Cow and Elephant Are Bad Friends

BEAT THE STORY-DRUM, *pum-pum!* Tell us a big story, *brum-brum!* The one about Elephant and Bush Cow, *thrum-thrum!* And of Monkey the messenger, *pittipong-pittipong!*

Bush Cow and Elephant were always bad friends. There was good reason why they didn't get along and could never settle their disputes.

Elephant was big, so was Bush Cow. They were nicknamed the Big Ones. They walked big, *brum-brum!* and talked big, *thrum-thrum!* It was the big, bad talk that got them into trouble, *pittipong-pittipong!*

Elephant liked to boast about his strength to everyone. He talked himself up and never missed making a slight or a put-down about Bush Cow's strength.

When Bush Cow heard that Elephant was bad-mouthing him, he felt ashamed and angry. He knew he was a good fighter and he feared no one. He told the tale-bearers a thing or two to take back to Elephant, *brum-brum!*

Wherever Bush Cow and Elephant walked, everyone stepped aside, no question about that. But because of the bad words that flew back and forth between them, neither Bush Cow nor Elephant would give way to the other. So whenever they met, they fought, *pum-pum!*

One day the Big Ones met on their way to market.

"Step aside and let me pass Bush Cow-ard," said Elephant, "or I'll braid your horns, *brum-brum!*"

"Out of my way, Snake Snout," said Bush Cow, "or I'll tie your trunk into knots, *thrum-thrum!*"

Greetings like that were bound to lead to blows. Elephant landed an opening clout; Bush Cow answered with a cuff; and then the bout was in full swing.

Bush Cow butted Elephant in his side. Elephant tripped Bush Cow with his trunk. They tumbled and tussled all over the field, pummeling each other as they rolled, *pum-pum! pum-pum!*

A crowd gathered. The village elders were distraught when they saw the torn-up field. They called out:

"Stop, stop! You're ruining the crop! Aie-yaie. It is as the proverb says: 'When two big ones fight, it is the grass that suffers.' Monkey, get closer and tell them to stop."

Monkey leaped into the tree nearest the fighters. He hung from the branches and chattered:

"Don't fee fa foo fight. It's not bee ba doo right."

Monkey's scat-talk was understood by everyone, but the Big Ones wouldn't listen to him. They kept on fighting.

Finally the Head Chief arrived and stopped the fight, for when the Head Chief commands, everyone obeys.

"What is happening here?" the Head Chief demanded.
Monkey hopped to him with his report:

"A fee fa foo fight. No bah ba dee body won. No nee na no
noo, not one of the two. Not Bush Cow, I know. Not Elephant
O. Wee why wo do they fight? What fee fa foo for? Their wee
ba ree bop heads are hard as a door. It's always a draw."

"Door, draw!" said Elephant. "Suppose he hadn't stuck me
with those horns, hah! I would have won, *thrum-thrum!*"

"Won, when!" said Bush Cow. "Suppose he hadn't tied my
fists with his trunk, I would have flattened him, *brum-brum!*"

"Suppose, suppose," cried the Head Chief in disgust. "Suppose your head was a door post!"

Everyone laughed.

"But suppose," said the Big Ones, who were not laughing, "suppose we let you settle this dispute between us. We can't."

The Head Chief looked at the field and knew that something had to be done. He conferred with the village elders then announced the plan:

"Elephant and Bush Cow will meet to fight in the large open space of the marketplace next market day, *thrum-thrum!* This dispute will be settled then, once and for all, *brum-brum!* Everyone from country and town is invited to come and witness the battle, *pum-pum!*"

The Big Ones agreed, and all the details of the Battle of the Big Ones were settled. Then the villagers went on their way to the beat of the drums, *prum-prum, thrum-thrum, pum-pum, pittipong-pittipong!*

When market day of the fight dawned, Bush Cow rose early. He wanted to be the first one there to prove he was no coward. He limbered up quickly then lumbered along the main road. He heard that Elephant had not yet passed that way so he took up his position on the road to market at some distance from town.

Bush Cow blocked the road and waited. He became impatient and began bellowing and tearing up the ground, *brum-brum!*

"What have you done with Big Big One? Have you seen him? Where is he?" he cried to everyone who passed.

Monkey came along the road and was stopped and questioned.

"How should I na nee know of bee ba ba ray Big Big One?" said Monkey. "I'm a lee ba lu bay little monkey. But don't wa wu wait here. Sha ba dee boo no. Go on to the square. Chief a ree bop said oo soo bee doo fight there."

Bush Cow let Monkey pass, but he paid no attention to what he said. He stood right where he was. He stopped Doe, Zebra and Wild Boar with the same question before he heard Elephant trumpeting in the bush, *thrum-thrum!*

Elephant was breaking down trees and trampling the bushes in his way. That's how he kept in form for the fight. He came onto the main road to market. There stood Bush Cow, blocking the way.

"Move on to the square," said Elephant. "We agreed to fight there."

Bush Cow didn't like Elephant's tone of voice, so he stood his ground and glared at him.

"Move! Move Bush Cow-ard!" said Elephant.

"Move me then Snake Snout!" said Bush Cow.

"O me ma moo my," said Monkey. "Don't fee foo fight here. Move oo bee doo on to the square."

The Big Ones brushed Monkey aside. They didn't want to listen, and they didn't waste words. They lowered their heads and charged, *powf!* That was the end of their promise to fight in the marketplace.

A tremendous battle began. The Big Ones pitched, rolled and tossed, damaging the nearby farms. The villagers were frightened from going on to market and hid out of harm's way, hoping the havoc would soon halt. The village elders were shocked when they came on the scene. They couldn't believe the Big Ones would disobey the Head Chief's battle plan.

"Monkey," they said, "quick! Run and tell the Head Chief all that is happening here."

Monkey had watched the fight from the start so he knew the message. He set off quickly, swinging through the branches and squealing as he swung. When he stopped a moment to catch his breath, he could no longer remember why he was in such a hurry, where he was going and what he was to say to whom, which is the forgetful way that monkeys have.

"Now why, where, to who, what for?" he asked himself. "What, where, why, to who? Shoo bee do, shoo bee do!"

Monkey danced, "Hay baa ba ree bop, hay baa . . ." Suddenly the message sprang back into his mind.

"Skoo bee do, skoo bee do," he sang in delight. He went on as fast as he could go so that he would not forget the message again.

When Monkey reached the Head Chief's house he remembered, "Shoo bee do" and "skoo bee do," but nothing more. He hadn't the slightest idea why he had come.

Well, he had arrived and that was something. He could at least act as if he were about important business. Shoo bee do, shoo bee do! he'd look busy, yeah!

Monkey sat down and engaged in a minute personal inspection of his fur. A minute later whop! he jumped up onto the roof of the house, *pittipong-pittipong!* He caught and ate a bug, then down he swung again to the ground.

There he found a stone and he rolled it around, backward and forward, forward and back, in an aimless sort of way while looking in the opposite direction.

Monkey soon tired of this and picked up a stick. He tapped out a rhythm on the stone, *whick, whack-a-whack; whick, whack-a-crack!* the stick broke. He flung the pieces into the bushes and flung the stone after them.

Monkey hopped onto the verandah and crouched with his head in his hands. He was almost at wit's end when his attention was attracted by a large praying mantis that fluttered past him into the Head Chief's house. It circled the room with a loud clatter of wings then settled on the floor and immediately assumed its usual prayerful attitude.

Monkey stalked the mantis carefully and was just about to seize it when the chief caught sight of him and shouted out in a loud voice:

"Ha, Monkey, is that you?"

At the sound of the Head Chief's voice, Monkey did a back flip and mantis flapped out the front door.

"Who, who?" cried Monkey. "O ya you no me. Yes-siree, it's bee ba dee me."

"What brings you here?" asked the chief.

"To see shoo bee do you. Yeah!"

Monkey cocked his head to one side, trying to look as if he had something wise to add to that. Actually he was thinking of nothing. He began chattering nervously about sticks and stones and mantis bones because everything else had gone out of his head, *pittipong-pittipong!*

"Well" said the Head Chief "if you've nothing more on your mind than that, then help yourself to one of the ripe bananas hanging up in the verandah."

Monkey was very fond of bananas and didn't need to be told twice. He went quickly and chose a large one, then returned to the room. Monkey peeled the banana and bit first one end, then the other, as if that would make it last longer. He studied the banana carefully after each bite.

"Monkey," said the Head Chief, "shouldn't Bush Cow and Elephant be here by now? I've been waiting for them all morning. They promised to meet in the market square for the big battle today."

Yoweee! Monkey somersaulted and came down chattering: "O sure shoo bee do, sure, sure shoo bee do!"

Monkey swallowed the last bit of banana, and after all sorts of scat-talk, squeals and grimaces told the Head Chief all of the elder's message.

"Aha!" said the Head Chief, "so that's why the market is almost empty today. Thanks for the message, Monkey. Help yourself to another banana. As for Bush Cow and Elephant, I'll see to it that they get theirs, *thrum-thrum!*"

Monkey ate the banana, pleased and impressed with himself. He was sure that there were not many others who could manage a message to match his style, shoo bee do, shoo bee do!

The Head Chief called for his bow and arrows, and Monkey led him to the scene of the battle. When the Head Chief arrived and saw the ruined farmlands, he didn't ask questions and he didn't raise his voice. Instead, he raised his arm with the bow and shot first one arrow, then another, *plung, plung!*

Bush Cow felt a sharp stab in his rump, *wow!*

Elephant felt a sharp stab in his rump, *wow!*

The Head Chief didn't wait. He shot a second volley of arrows and prepared to shoot a third.

But Bush Cow and Elephant got the message. They didn't wait for any more arrows to fly. They flew! They plunged into the bush and disappeared, *brum-brum!*

After that the Head Chief refused to have anything more to do with settling disputes between Bush Cow and Elephant. But ever since then, when wild animals fight, they always fight in the bush and not on public roads, *thrum-thrum!*

Since the big battle between Bush Cow and Elephant was never decided, each still boasts that he is the stronger. Whenever they meet along main roads, they argue. Whenever they meet in the bush, they fight.

So to this day, *pum-pum!* Bush Cow and Elephant, *thrum-thrum!* remain bad friends, *brum-brum!*

Pittipong-pittipong!

The Husband Who Counted the Spoonfuls

ONCE THERE WAS a man named Tagwayi, as stubborn in his way as stone, but gentle as a leaf. He was a good man and good-looking, too. He had no trouble getting a wife, but he did have trouble keeping one.

Tagwayi couldn't stay married because he always counted the spoonfuls.

It wasn't only spoonfuls that Tagwayi counted. He counted everything he saw on his walks through the village and as he worked in his fields. He counted huts, people, chickens, trees and the rows he'd hoed in his field, all with equal enthusiasm. He loved the rhythm of counting and the sound of numbers.

Tagwayi counted for pleasure and not out of envy or greed.

The villagers admired Tagwayi's skill with numbers. He was often called in by the village elders to help resolve difficult number matters. But to count the spoonfuls of food served was considered a disgrace by all, as bad as knocking the spoonful of food out of another's mouth. No wife would stay married to a husband with such a rude habit.

Because of this, Tagwayi's first wife had left him, then the second and the third. Each time that Tagwayi married, he would manage to control his urge to count the spoonfuls for a week or two. Then he'd lose control and sing out the spoonfuls count.

"That does it!" the wife would say. "You did it! Good-bye!"

And the wife would go, leaving Tagwayi alone.

The villagers made up a song about him:

"He's a counting the spoonfuls, no'count,

  Can't keep a wife.

  A counting the spoonfuls, no'count,

  Hungry for life."

There was no telling how many wives Tagwayi had driven out with this stubborn habit. The villagers said: "More than you could shake a stick at!" As much as Tagwayi liked to count, he was too ashamed to keep count of his past wives. He'd had so many, and now he hadn't any.

He crouched in his hut by the burned pot of food he'd fixed. Rocking on his heels, he'd moan and lament for all to hear, but there was no wife there.

"Aie-yaie," he cried. "Here am I! What? Me one, all alone in this hut! Eh, eh? Don't I too need a wife?"

71

Tagwayi mumbled and muttered and talked crazy talk to the cooking pot, but talk didn't change the pot into a wife. Then he recalled the proverb: "The journey is on the road, it doesn't rest in the mouth."

Tagwayi stood up and counted his steps—one, two, three, four—that brought him to the door of his hut. Then five, six, seven, eight, nine, ten, eleven that got him across the compound. Twelve, thirteen, fourteen steps sped him on his way. Fifteen, sixteen, seventeen took him along the path that led to the villages beyond.

Tagwayi walked along kicking the spear-grass as he went. A hornbill alighted in a tree branch overhead and sang: "Chilin, chilin! chilin, chilin!" Tagwayi listened and counted the calls to feel the thrill of it all the more deeply. Ah! There was a good round count to the song. He was sure now that he would find a wife.

And he did, even though it meant traveling further than he'd ever traveled before.

"Today's a happy day," he sang. "I've found a wife."

"Chilin, chilin! Chilin, chilin!" echoed the hornbill.

Tagwayi couldn't wait to bring his wife to his compound. He took her hand.

"Let's go!" he said.

"Shouldn't we wait till morning? You might lose the way after dark."

"Oh no!" said Tagwayi. "I know the way, and later the moon will help us. Besides, it is said, 'Even in the dark, the hand that holds food does not lose its way to the mouth.' "

Tagwayi set out with his wife, and he had no trouble finding the way home by moonlight.

Now he was a happy man. Every morning, on his way to work in his fields, he made up a numbers song:

"Take two out of ten
 Split twelve for the four
 Add thirty threes
 To nine nineties
 Times six. Then halve the score."

The villagers heard him singing as he passed. They knew that although Tagwayi counted all the time, he sang his number songs only when he was very happy. He had a wife, she was a good cook and he ate well. They noticed a slight skip in his step as he kept time to the number tune.

When Tagwayi returned home from work in the fields, he watched his wife pound, winnow and wash the corn. He counted the number of times she repeated this until the corn flour was fine enough for the evening meal of tuwo. And when his wife poured the miya sauce over the tuwo he sang:

"The world's a pleasant place
 for two who eat tuwo."

"Chilin, chilin," sang the hornbill.

As his wife dished the tuwo into the calabashes Tagwayi asked; "What is the number for today?"

"What number foolishness is this you're asking about?"

"Uh-uh." Tagwayi laughed. "You won't catch me counting the spoonfuls. I've learned well that 'Whoever mounts the horse of Had-I-But-Known suffers trouble'!"

Tagwayi's wife spooned on, but it was a close call. After that he stepped outside whenever food was being dished out. He'd count trees, he'd count stones, he'd count butterflies and cries of the hornbill, "Chilin, chilin." And when he came in, he wasn't tempted to count at all, not one spoonful.

Two weeks passed, then three. One night Tagwayi circled the hut. He felt hungrier than ever, and he counted faster than ever, too. He counted himself out and was ready to enter too soon.

The hornbill alighted on the ground nearby and cried in warning: "Woh, woh! woh woh!"

Tagwayi said, "Woh, woh? No, no! Sing chilin, chilin!" But the hornbill sang, "Woh, woh!" again.

He didn't heed the warning and rushed into the hut. His wife had just begun to dish out the tuwo. Tagwayi squatted down beside her.

"One-a-spoonful, two-a-spoonful, three-a-spoonful, four," he began.

His wife was annoyed. She drew in her breath and sucked her teeth, "Choops." Tagwayi didn't notice a thing.

"Five, six, seven, eight, add a spoonful more."

"Choops, choops," choopsed his wife, but even her choopsing didn't get through to him. He couldn't stop counting.

"Nine spoonfuls, ten spoonfuls. Will not come again spoonfuls."

"And neither will I!" cried his wife. She klonked him on the head with the spoon and left.

The klonk brought Tagwayi back to his senses, but it was too late. His counting spoonfuls had driven out his wife again.

"Ah! This time I have fallen into the cooking pot," he said.

"Woh, woh! Woh, woh!" echoed the hornbill.

The next day Tagwayi walked around the village hoping to hear news that might lead him to a new wife. As he made the rounds, so did the song:

"He's a counting the spoonfuls, no'count,
Can't keep a wife
A counting the spoonfuls, no'count,
Hungry for life."

Tagwayi was left with the days to count as they passed. His cooking didn't improve, and sometimes he burned the tuwo two or three nights in a row. Counting the spoonfuls hardly made up for that.

One day the hornbill sang again: "Chilin, chilin!" It was the day that Tagwayi heard about a woman who was the fairest in her town. He set off at once to her home to seek her in marriage.

"I have heard of you," she said.

"Oh," said Tagwayi. He knew what she must have heard. "Then you won't be my wife?"

"Chilin, chilin," sang the hornbill.

"We-ell," she said, "I'm not refusing you."

"You will then," he cried. "Oh, the world's once again a happy place!"

"Now listen Tagwayi so you won't have to mount the horse of Had-I-But-Known. If I marry you, there is one thing that will cause us to separate."

"Uh . . . er . . . what um . . . er . . . ah's that?"

"Your only failing is counting spoonfuls," she said. "Count sheep, count corn, count cowries. Count what you will, but in good health or ill, don't count spoonfuls!"

"Well," said Tagwayi, "if that's all there is to it, I promise I won't do it again. Since you say that is what you do not like, I'll see to it that I stay out of the cooking pot with you."

"Very well," she said.

So they were married, and Tagwayi brought his new wife to live in his compound.

The months passed. Every day Tagwayi went to work in his fields and sang his curious number songs. When he returned home, the hornbill sang in a tree outside the hut: "Chilin, chilin! Chilin, chilin!" The villagers no longer teased Tagwayi with their "Counting the spoonfuls, no'count" song. It seemed that at last he was well married.

During those months Tagwayi did as before. He counted outdoors until the meals were spooned into the calabashes. He kept to the proverb: "When the eye does not see, the heart does not grieve."

One day, as the hornbill sang, "Chilin, chilin!" Tagwayi hit on a new idea, a way to control his stubborn habit. He counted silently outdoors. After weeks of practice, he became so good at it that he no longer moved his lips. True, he did bat his eyelids and tap with a big toe for each count, but that was hardly noticeable.

Now he could sit indoors while his wife served the meals; his silent counting-the-spoonfuls system worked.

"Chilin, chilin!" sang the hornbill.

Tagwayi's wife was so pleased that he'd given up that stone-stubborn habit that she'd spoon in extra spoonfuls for him.

One evening Tagwayi sat on the edge of the bed, counting

spoonfuls silently as his wife spooned out the tuwo. He batted his eyelids and tapped his toe to:

"One, two, in you go. Three, four and many more. Five, six delicious licks. Seven eight . . ."

Just then a neighbor called from the entrance to the compound:

"Hey Tagwayi!"

"Nine!" answered Tagwayi.

His wife paid no attention, she didn't even say choops. She just went on spooning out the tuwo.

Tagwayi talked with the caller, but he never took his eyes off the pot. The hornbill flew down to the ground and warned, "Woh, woh! Woh, woh!" but Tagwayi didn't hear.

His wife had reached eleven spoonfuls and was about to dish out the twelfth when Tagwayi came back in.

"If I hadn't told you that I had given up counting the spoonfuls," he said, "I should say that you have just put the twelfth spoonful into the calabash."

"You did it just now," she cried. "When you said 'nine,' I pretended not to hear, for I thought you had just forgotten. But no, you are back to your old rotten tricks."

"Old rotten tricks?" said Tagwayi. "Did you hear me count to twelve? Uh, it was twelve spoonfuls you dished out though, wasn't it?"

"Dished out, fished out!" cried his wife. "Now who's counting the spoonfuls?" She dropped the spoon on Tagwayi's big toe. "I'm not living with a husband who counts spoonfuls!"

The next morning his wife left.

"Count the grass!" she cried as she went, and she never returned to his compound.

"Woh, woh!" mourned the hornbill.

That was the last of the many wives that Tagwayi had. After that he never got another wife. He sat where his last wife left him and counted. And since it is the grass he counts, Tagwayi is counting still.

Why Frog and Snake Never Play Together

MAMA FROG had a son. Mama Snake also had a son. One morning both children went out to play.

Mama Snake called after her child:

"Watch out for big things with sharp claws and teeth that gnaw. Don't lose your way in the bush, baby, and be back to the burrow before dark."

"Clawsangnaws," sang Snake as he went looping through the grass. "Beware of the Clawsangnaws."

Mama Frog called after her son:

"Watch out for things that peck or bite. Don't go into the bush alone, dear. Don't fight, and get home before night."

"Peckorbite," sang Frog as he went hopping from stone to stone. "Beware of the Peckorbite!"

Snake was singing his Clawsangnaws song, and Frog was singing of Peckorbites when they met along the way. They had never met before.

"Who are you?" asked Frog. "Are you a Peckorbite?" and he prepared to spring out of reach.

"Oh no! I'm Snake, called by my Mama 'Snakeson': I'm slick, lithe and slithery. Who are you? Are you a Clawsangnaws?" and he got ready to move, just in case.

"No no! I'm Frog, called by my Mama 'Frogchild.' I'm hip, quick and hoppy."

They stood and stared at each other, then they said together: "You don't look anything like me."

Their eyes brightened. They did not look alike, that's true, but some of their customs were alike. Both knew what to do when two say the same thing at the same time.

They clasped each other, closed their eyes and sang:

> "You wish a wish
> I'll wish a wish, too;
> May your wish and my wish
> Both come true."

Each made a wish then let go.

Just then a fly flew by, right past Frog's eyes. Flip! out went his tongue as he flicked in the fly.

A bug whizzed past snake's nose. Flash! Snake flicked out his tongue and caught the bug.

They looked in admiration at each other and smiled. The two new friends now knew something of what each other could do. They felt at ease with each other, like old friends.

"Let's play!" said Frog.

"Hey!" said Snake, "that was my wish. Let's play in the bush."

"The bush! In the bush!" cried Frog. "That was my wish. If you go with me, it's all right 'cause Mama said I shouldn't go alone."

Frog and Snake raced to the bush and started playing games.

"Watch this," said Frog. He crouched down and counted, "One a fly, two a fly, three a fly, four!"

He popped way up into the air, somersaulted and came down, whop!

"Can you do that Snake?"

Snake bounded for a nearby mound to try the Frog-Hop. He got to the top of the slope, stood on the tip of his tail and tossed himself into the air. Down he came, flop! a tangle of coils. He laughed and tried again.

Sometimes Snake and Frog jumped together and bumped in midair. No matter how hard they hit, it didn't hurt. They had fun.

Then Snake said, "Watch this!" He stretched out at the top of the mound and counted, "One a bug, two a bug, three a bug, four!" Then swoosh! he slithered down the slope on his stomach.

"Try that Frog. It's called the Snake-Slither."

Frog lay on his stomach and slipped down the hill. His arms and legs flailed about as he slithered. He turned over at the bottom of the slope, *blump!* and rolled up in a lump.

Frog and Snake slithered down together, entangling as they went. Their calls and laughter could be heard all over the bush. One game led to another. They were having such a good time that the day passed swiftly. By late afternoon there were not two better friends in all the bush.

The sun was going down when Snake remembered his promise to his mother.

"I promised to be home before dark," he said.

"Me too," said Frog. "Good-bye!"

They hugged. Snake was so happy that he'd found a real friend that he forgot himself and squeezed Frog very tightly. It felt good, very, very good.

"Ow! easy!" said Frog. "Not too tight."

"Oh, sorry," said Snake loosening his hug-hold. "My! but you sure feel good, good enough to eat."

At that they burst out laughing and hugged again, lightly this time.

"I like you," said Frog. "Bye, Snake."

"Bye, Frog. You're my best friend."

"Let's play again tomorrow," they said together.

Aha! they clasped and sang once again:

> *"You wish a wish*
> *I'll wish a wish, too;*
> *May your wish and my wish*
> *Both come true."*

Off they went, Snake hopping and Frog slithering all the way home.

When Frog reached home, he knocked his knock, and Mama Frog unlocked the rock door. She was startled to see her child come slithering in across the floor.

"Now what is this, eh?" she said. "Look at you, all covered with grass and dirt."

"It doesn't hurt," said Frog. "I had fun."

"Fun? Now what is this, eh? I can tell you haven't been playing in ponds or bogs with the good frogs. Where have you been all day? You look as if you've just come out of the bush."

"But I didn't go alone, Ma. I went with a good boy. He's my best friend."

"Best friend? Now what is this, eh?" said Mama Frog. "What good boy could that be, playing in the bush?"

"Look at this trick that he taught me, Ma," said Frogchild. He flopped on his stomach and wriggled across the floor, bungling up Mama Frog's neatly stitched lily-pad rug.

"That's no trick for a frog! Get up from there, child!" cried Mama Frog. "Now what is this, eh?" Look how you've balled up my rug. Just you tell me, who was this playmate?"

"His name is Snakeson, Mama."

"Snake, son! Did you say Snake, son?"

"Yes. What's the matter, Mama?"

Mama Frog trembled and turned a pale green. She sat down to keep from fainting. When she had recovered herself, she said:

"Listen Frogchild, listen carefully to what I have to say." She pulled her son close. "Snake comes from the Snake family. They are bad people. Keep away from them. You hear me, child?"

"Bad people?" asked Frog.

"Bad, too bad!" said Mama Frog. "Snakes are sneaks. They hide poison in their tongues, and they crush you in their coils."

Frogchild gulped.

"You be sure to hop out of Snake's reach if ever you meet again. And stop this slithering foolishness. Slithering's not for frogs."

Mama Frog set the table muttering to herself: "Playing with Snake! Now what is this, eh?" She rolled a steaming ball of gleaming cornmeal onto Frogchild's plate.

"Sit down and eat your funji, child," said Mama Frog. "And remember, I'm not fattening frogs for snakes, eh?"

Snake too reached home. He rustled the braided twig hatch-cover to his home. His mother knew his rustle and undid the vine latch. Snake toppled in.

"I'm hungry, Ma," he said, hopping all about.

"Eh, eh! Do good bless you! What a sight you are!" said Mama Snake. "Just look at you. And listen to your panting and wheezing. Where have you been all day?"

"In the bush, Mama, with my new friend. We played games. See what he taught me."

Snakeson jumped up on top of the table and leaped into the air. He came down on a stool, knocking it over and entangling himself in its legs.

"Eh, eh! Do good bless you. What a dangerous game that is," said Mama Snake. "Keep it up and see if you don't break every bone in your back. What new friend taught you that?"

She bent over and untangled her son from the stool.

"My frog friend taught me that. His name's Frogchild. It's the Frog-Hop Mama. Try it. It's fun."

"Frog, child?" Mama Snake's jaws hung open showing her fangs. "Did you say Frog, child?"

"Yes," said Snakeson. "He's my best friend."

"You mean you played all day with a frog and you come home hungry?"

"He was hungry too, Mama, after playing the Snake Slither game that I taught him."

"Eh, eh! Well do good bless you! Come, curl up here son and listen carefully to what I have to tell you."

Snakeson curled up on the stool.

"Don't you know, son, that it is the custom of our house to eat frogs? Frogs are delicious people!"

Snakeson's small eyes widened.

"Ah, for true!" said Mama Snake. "Eating frogs is the custom of our house, a tradition in our family. Hopping isn't, so cut it out, you hear me?"

"Oh, Mama," cried Snakeson. "I can't eat frogs. Frog's a friend."

"Frog a friend! Do good bless you!" said Mama Snake. "That's not natural. Now you listen to me, baby. The next time you play with Frog, jump roll and romp all you like. But when you get hungry, his game is up. Catch him and eat him!"

The next morning Snakeson was up early. He pushed off his dry-leaf cover and stretched himself. He remembered his mother's words, and the delicious feel of his frog friend when they had hugged. He was ready to go.

Mama Snake fixed her son a light breakfast of spiced insects and goldfinch eggs. Snakeson was soon on his way.

"Now don't you forget my instructions about frogs, do good bless you," Mama Snake called out after him. "And don't let me have to tell you again to watch out for big things with sharp claws and teeth that gnaw."

"Clawsangnaw," sang Snakeson. "Clawsangnaw."

He reached the bush and waited for his friend. He looked forward to fun with Frog, and he looked forward to finishing the fun with a feast of his fine frog friend. He lolled about in the sun, laughing and singing:

> "You wish a wish
> I'll wish a wish, too;
> Can your wish and my wish
> Both come true?"

The sun rose higher and higher, but Frog did not come.

"What's taking Frogchild so long," said Snakeson. "Perhaps too much slithering has given him the bellyache. I'll go and look for him."

Snake found Frog's rock home by the pond. He rolled up a stone in his tail and knocked on the rock door.

"Anybody home?"

"Just me," answered Frogchild.

"May I come in?"

"Ah, it's you Snakeson. Sorry, my Mama's out, and she said not to open the door to anyone."

"Come on out then and let's play," said Snakeson. "I waited all morning for you in the bush."

"I can't," said Frog, "not now, anyway."

"Oh, that's too bad," said Snake. "My mother taught me a new game. I'd love to teach it to you."

"I'll bet you would," said Frog.

"You don't know what you're missing," said Snake.

"But I do know what you're missing," said Frog, and he burst out laughing.

"Aha!" said Snake. "I see that your mother has given you instructions. My mother has given me instructions too."

Snake sighed. There was nothing more to say or do, so he slithered away.

Frog and Snake never forgot that day when they played together as friends. Neither ever again had that much fun with anybody.

Today you will see them, quiet and alone in the sun, still as stone. They are deep in thought remembering that day of games in the bush, and both of them wonder:

"What if we had just kept on playing together, and no one had ever said anything?"

But from that day to this, Frog and Snake have never played together again.

You wish a wish
I'll wish a wish, too;
May your wish and my wish
Both come true.

How Animals Got Their Tails

IF YOU'RE TALKING about the beginning of things, you've got to go back, way, way back, back to the time when the animals had no tails.

That's right! In the beginning Raluvhimba, god of the Bavenda, created the animals without tails. Uh-huh! He never even gave tails a thought, uh-uh! not in the beginning.

When Raluvhimba came down from the heavens, he often sat in his favorite place on earth, high on Mount Tsha-wa-dinda. He'd relax there and admire the world that he had made: the mountains, rivers and trees, the sun, moon and stars.

"Uh-huh!" he'd say to himself, for in the beginning there was no one to uh-huh to. "Uh-huh! That sure looks good."

One day on Mount Tsha-wa-dinda, Raluvhimba lay down in Cave Luvhimbi and fell asleep. He dreamed a dream of animals that wandered the earth. And when he awoke, he set to work.

One by one Raluvhimba made the animals: Elephant and Mouse, Rabbit and Rhinoceros, Monkey and Ox, Lion and Fox. The large and the small, he made them all.

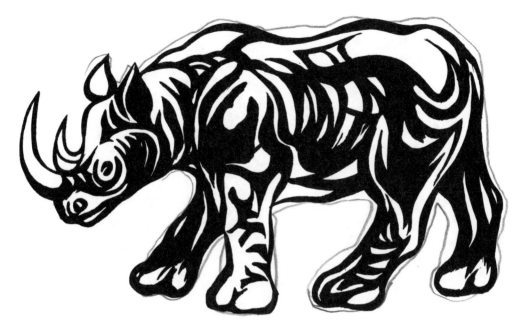

Raluvhimba worked hard to get each one right, Lion's first mane tripped him up, had to be shortened. Goats first coat was too tight a fit, had to be loosened. It took two tusks to complete Elephant, and it took a tusk or two to do Rhinoceros's snout.

Mouse was the last and the smallest of the creatures that Raluvhimba made.

"Uh-huh!" he said, holding Mouse in the palm of his hand. "How's that for small?"

"Uh-huh!" they all chanted back. "Small and beautiful."

But big or small, the animals had no color at all. So Raluvhimba mixed colors from the dye of plants. He took some leftover bristles from Hog and made a brush. Then he painted all the animals. Some he painted in plain colors, others he daubed with spots, and on some he painted stripes.

"Now you're complete," he said. "Uh-huh! You sure look good."

In those days no people were around. Raluvhimba hadn't yet thought of making man, so the animals had no one to fear. They roamed everywhere freely and fed on plants, shrubs and greens. They had good appetites, and they had good manners. They never even thought of eating each other. Uh-uh! Not in those days. They were vegetarians. The lion lay down with the lamb, and they all lived together peacefully.

Everywhere that Raluvhimba walked on earth there were animals to greet him. He was never without company on earth, and he liked that. But his trips through water and air were lonely; nobody in the water, nobody in the air.

Raluvhimba slept again in Cave Luvhimbi, and this time he dreamed of creatures for the water, creatures for the air.

He awoke and fleshed fish with scales to flash through the seas. He feathered birds for flight and tuned their voices to sing sweet songs.

"Uh-huh" cheered the animals. "That's some creating! It sure looks good!"

Now Raluvhimba had friends everywhere. Things couldn't have been better on earth, in the air or in the sea.

When he swam through the depths of the sea, the fish said "Lo!" as they saw him go. When he soared way up in the sky, the birds sang "Hi!" as he flew by. When he walked on earth, the animals said, "Pleasant day," as he passed their way, and they wiggled their ears for, as you remember, in those days the animals had no tails to waggle.

One day Raluvhimba played with the animals on Mount Tsha-wa-dinda. They liked seeing him make things so they circled him and chanted:

"O Creator create
Make something new,
Smaller than Mouse
And alive, too."

"Give it fine fur," said Fox.

"Mark it with stripes," said Zebra.

"Don't forget long ears," said Rabbit. "It will need long ears to wiggle."

Raluvhimba laughed. He closed his eyes and rubbed his forehead. An idea flickered. His fingers spun swiftly in space. Then he cupped his hands and blew into them. When he opened them, ahh! there stood Spider, alive and spinning.

"Oh, yeah! Now that is small," said Rabbit, "smaller than Mouse. No long ears, but he's sure got a lot of legs."

The animals crowded around and counted.

"One, two, three, four more than ours. Five, six more than birds. Seven, eight more than fish."

"Oh, eight legs, eight,
And ain't none of them straight."

Spider spun a strand from Raluvhimba's fingers and dropped all the way down to the ground, *pim!* unhurt.

"Do it!" said the animals.

"Uh-huh!" said Spider, and he twirled back up the strand into Raluvhimba's hand.

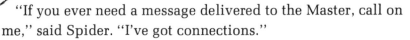

"If you ever need a message delivered to the Master, call on me," said Spider. "I've got connections."

Spider's tie to Raluvhimba made him feel as important as Rabbit felt about his long ears. Raluvhimba was pleased that Spider was accepted by the animals as one of them. He decided to create more tiny creatures.

This time Raluvhimba made Fly and his mate, and they multiplied rapidly. And with insects came trouble.

At first flies fed on plant juice and dew as Spider did. But between meals they'd sit uninvited on the animals. Now Spider never did that; and even though Fly was light, the animals didn't like being sat on.

"Don't sit on me," said Rabbit.

"Go live on a tree," said Zebra.

"Take your big feet out of my mouth," said Ox.

So it went, day after day. One day when Fly was living high on the hog, he got fed up with all the complaints and took a bite out of Hog's hide. To his surprise he liked the taste. He bit again to make sure, then flew about tasting a few more hides.

"Umm, not bad," said Fly. "Tastier too than plant juice or dew."

Fly told a friend, "If you want a meal with body to it . . ." and word got around. Soon flies were tasting every animal in sight and sharing their best ideas for beast feasts.

"Try this," said Fly. "Taste Lion first, then take a bite of Deer, and finish with a nip of Rabbit. Dee-licious!"

The animals howled when bitten, they shook when tickled, they flinched when pinched. Suddenly one would leap up into the air, another would roll on the ground, another rub vigorously against a tree. Everyone knew why. The fault was Fly.

Finally the animals could stand it no longer. They called for Spider and asked if he would take a message to Raluvhimba.

"What's the message?" asked Spider.

"Flies are pests! Tell Raluvhimba that flies are not fit friends for animals. They're flesh-biters and blood-suckers. Tell him to take them back."

Spider didn't waste time. He tested a few strands and found one that led into the heavens.

"Aha, so it's you Spider," said Raluvhimba. "I thought I felt a tiny tug at my toe."

"Lo!" said Spider. He didn't waste time in greetings. "I've a message for you from the animals. They say flies are pests; they bite and they chew us, yes, that's what they do, and we don't want them around."

"What?" said Raluvhimba. "I can't take back what I've given. After all, that's life. Don't flies chew leaves for juice and suck dew as you do?"

"Oh, no, uh-uh, no!" said Spider. "Flies bite flesh and suck blood. That's the message. They're not fit friends for us. You've got to do something to help and fast. I play Free-the-Fly with them when they get caught in my web so I'm fine, but my friends are frantic."

Raluvhimba thought, "I can't believe that flies are a flaw in my creation."

But there it was, almost in the beginning. A small mistake uh-huh, a tiny one true, but a bad sign just the same, and man hadn't even been created yet.

"Listen Spider," said Raluvhimba, "instead of playing Free-the-Fly, suppose you ate the flies that stuck to your web?"

"Oo-oo," groaned Spider. The very idea made him sick. He was, after all, a vegetarian and had never even thought of eating fly meat.

"Stop groaning, Spider," said Raluvhimba. "I've a better idea. I'll make tails for animals to flick away the flies."

Spider sang:

> *"Birds have tails*
> *Fish have tails*
> *The bird tail whishes*
> *The fish tail swishes.*
> *When's our day*
> *For tail's with which*
> *To flick and switch*
> *The flies away?"*

"Today's Moon Day," said Raluvhimba. "Tell the animals I'll come down to Mount Tsha-wa-dinda tomorrow and make tails for all of them."

"Good," said Spider. "Today's Moon Day. Tomorrow's Choose Day. Choose Day's Tails Day."

Spider descended quickly and spread the word. When the animals heard the good news, they couldn't wait to choose a tail. They set out at once for Mount Tsha-wa-dinda. Only Rabbit, who was very lazy, went back to sleep.

"Get going, Long Ears," said Spider. "I know you heard the message."

"I don't see you going anywhere either," said Rabbit.

"I don't need a tail, but you do," said Spider.

"What's the rush?" said Rabbit. "There's lots of time, and there'll be lots of tails."

"Uh-huh," said Spider.

Rabbit yawned and fell asleep.

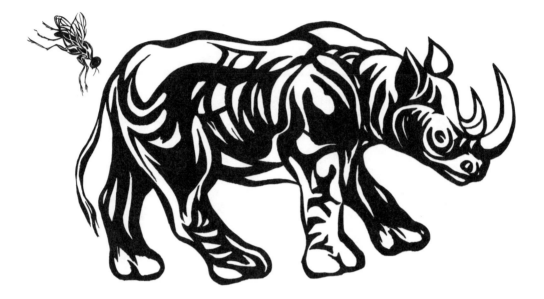

The next day Rabbit awoke to see animals passing by his burrow, wearing the most wonderful tails. Whenever a fly tried to land on an animal, it would swing its tail swoosh, swish, flick, and the fly would take off.

Animals with tails! A new scene on earth. Rabbit had to admit that it sure looked good. But even after his long rest, Rabbit was too lazy to stir himself.

"Who can I get to go for me," he thought. Then he saw Fox coming.

"Ah, Brother Fox," he said, "your tail is fantastic! Flies can't touch you now. I bet you run faster with it than you ever did before without it."

"Yeah!" said Fox. "This tail-piece does it. I'm fast now. I'm really fast."

"Brother Fox," said Rabbit, "since you're so much faster than I, would you run back and choose a fine tail for me?"

"Why sure, Brother Rabbit," said Fox, "be happy to do you the favor."

Fox sprang off, but he stopped to match tails with every animal he met along the way. It took him twice as long as it would have taken Rabbit to get there.

When Fox climbed up to Cave Luvhimbi, all the animals except Rabbit had already been there. He looked around and didn't see any tails at all. But as he turned to go, he spotted a short fur piece caught in the crevice of a rock.

"How stubby!" said Fox. "Can't flick flies much with that, but it's the only one left. Well, a long tail goes well with my short ears, so maybe a short tail will go well with long ears."

Fox took the tail and started back.

From his web in the high tree branches, Spider saw Fox approaching. He could make out only one bushy tail waving as Fox came closer. Spider said nothing of this when he dropped down beside Rabbit.

"Where's your tail?" asked Spider.

"Don't worry," said Rabbit. "It's coming."

Fox arrived and dropped the small fur ball before Rabbit.

"Here's your tail, Brother Rabbit," said Fox. "Not much of a tail, but it's all that was left. Still it is a tail, and that's the style nowadays."

Rabbit blinked his eyes.

"Here," said Fox, "let me help you put it on."

Rabbit was too stunned to move. Fox flipped him across his knees and tapped the tail into place. That done, Fox didn't wait around for thanks. He winked at Spider and ran off, laughing as he went.

Spider twirled back up to his web and sang under his breath:

*"Tails with which
to flick and switch
The flies away."*

Then he sang out loud and clear for Rabbit to hear:

"If you want a thing well done,
   go do it yourself. Uh-huh, uh-huh!"

But Spider's moral only made Rabbit madder.

"That Fox, that sly Fox!" he cried. "What took him so long, huh? That's why I came out on the short end of it. I'll get even with him!"

But that tale leads to other tales of Rabbit and Fox, and here's where this tale ends. For whether it's an animal's tail or a told tale, be it long or short, whatever the sort, all must come to an end.

Uh-huh!

Lion
and the
Ostrich Chicks

and Other African Folktales

Lion and the Ostrich Chicks

Once upon a time Papa and Mama Ostrich prepared to have a family. Papa Ostrich made a nest in the sand for Mama Ostrich. He swooped about and scooped out a shallow hollow. He smoothed over all the lumps and bumps. Then Mama ostrich stepped in, settled down and laid six eggs.

Mama and Papa Ostrich took turns sitting on the eggs, Mama by day, Papa by night. They warmed the eggs and watched and waited. One morning, six weeks later, six little ostrich chicks kicked their way out of their shells.

The parents circled round their children. They scuffed their two-toed feet in the sand and sang:

"Ostrich stretch, strut, stride and race.
Six little chicks just joined the chase.
Clap for Ostrich, one, two!
Stamp for Lion, shoo, shoo!"

Papa Ostrich boomed out the good news for all to hear. His deep lionlike roar startled the six little chicks. They ran to their Mama.

"Nothing to fear my chicks," said Mama Ostrich, hugging them to her. "That deep, hissing roar is your Papa's voice."

She brought them closer to Papa. The chicks listened as he sounded his deep, hissing roar again.

"That's our Papa," they chirped. "Well, all right, Papa!"

The chicks were so excited, they jumped into the air and fluttered their wings in flight. Down they tumbled to the ground.

"Two pretty little wings," said Mama Ostrich. "But too tiny to fly."

"Now don't you cry," said Papa Ostrich. "We can't fly high on our wings, but we sure can fly on our feet. Watch me!"

Papa Ostrich raced from a nearby bush to a distant tree and back.

"Uh-huh," he said. "Did you see my fleet feet fly? We're the only two-toed birds around, and we use our feet to cover ground."

Papa Ostrich taught the chicks his best running tricks. Every day the chicks practiced their steps: stretch, strut and stride. They got better and better and ran faster and faster.

Weeks passed and soon the chicks could outrun everyone around. They challenged Zebra and Hare and left them in the rear. They raced Deer and Fox and left them in the dust. They were fit and fast and always finished first. Finally they could even keep up with their parents.

"You're fast and that's fine," said Mama Ostrich. "But don't run off too far from home, not until you're fully grown and know your way around."

"We won't," they promised.

Each day the six chicks ran farther away from home, but they remembered their promise. They always turned back before they had gone too far.

One morning the chicks awoke before everyone else. They rose early to practice dashes, relays and sprints. Now that they had learned how to fly on their feet, they didn't miss wings at all.

"Let's go!" they cried.

Away they ran. They raced from their home to a nearby bush. They rushed past the bush to a distant tree. From the tree they chased to the hill beyond. Down the hill they sped, then around a pond. They flew on their feet to a field full of rocks. They leaped and they hopped and came to a stop. They fell on the ground and rolled around. They had run so far. They felt so proud. They laughed and gasped and caught their breath. "Ah . . . Whew! Ah . . . Whew!"

They'd had so much fun running, they hadn't given a thought to where they were going or how far they had gone. They looked around, and they didn't recognize anything.

"Where are we? We're lost! We're lost!" they cried.

Just then a reassuring, roaring sound came from behind the mound of rocks ahead.

"Papa! Mama!" they shouted. "Here we are!"

They ran as one to the mound of rocks and peered behind. Suddenly, shrump! Lion swept all six chicks into his den.

"Welcome home, children," Lion roared.

"You sound like Papa," the chicks said. "But you don't look like Papa at all. You're all fur, four feet and no feathers."

"I can stand on two feet, too, just like you," said Lion. "I'm your papa now."

Lion tapped their stomachs, hmm, and licked his lips, mmm!

"You must be tired, my little chicks," said Lion. "Now go to bed."

When their children didn't come home that day, Mama
and Papa Ostrich searched everywhere until it grew dark.
The chicks were nowhere around, nowhere to be found.

The next morning they set out early to ask if anyone
had seen their chicks.

Everyone said, "No," until Mama Ostrich asked
Mongoose.

"I was up early yesterday," said Mongoose, "and I saw them running. They ran from their home to a nearby bush. Then they ran from the bush to a distant tree. They raced from the tree to the trail up the hill. I saw them running with all their might till they crossed the hill and dropped out of sight. Now just past the hill there's a pond below. If they circled around and didn't fall into the pond, they were bound to come to the mound of rocks—where Lion lives. You don't suppose . . ."

Mama Ostrich's heart went flip-flop. She didn't wait for Mongoose to finish and she didn't stop to think or to thank Mongoose.

She rushed off, whish! past the nearby bush. She raced past the distant tree, whee! She sped on the trail up the hill beyond and she picked up speed as she circled the pond. Then she came to the mound of rocks, whoa! She stopped. Just ahead was Lion's den. Lion sat at the entrance guarding the chicks.

"My children!" Mama Ostrich cried when she saw her chicks.

The chicks hopped up and down.

"Your children? Uh-uh! My children!" said Lion.

"Anyone can see they're mine," said Mama Ostrich.

"Anyone is no one," said Lion. "And you'll need someone to stand up to me."

Mama Ostrich was confused by Lion's crafty talk, but

she wasn't confused about whose children Lion was claiming as his own.

"Stop that Ostrich-hop," Lion said to the chicks. "Do the lion cub crouch I taught you. If you step out of line, snip! I'll snap off your heads. You're lions now. Did you hear what I said?"

"Oh! Don't mistreat them," Mama Ostrich said. "And please don't eat them."

"Uh-uh!" said Lion. "Not now, anyway. But when they're fatter, that will be another matter. Now take off, you tall-necked, long-legged, two-toed, top-heavy bird!"

Lion bared his teeth and growled.

Mama Ostrich fled for help.

She found Papa Ostrich. They went together to tell their story to Chief Counselor Fox and the animal counselors. The counselors listened and agreed to help.

"A strange story, but a simple case," they said. "It's apparent that no true parent could possibly mix cubs and chicks."

"Uh-uh," said Papa Ostrich. "That's Lion's tricks, not Lion's chicks!"

"Oh, look!" said Mama Ostrich. "Here comes Lion now. He's walking my chicks!"

Lion came striding by, walking upright with the six chicks in tow. The counselors bowed politely to Lion.

"Meet my children," Lion said.

"Nice chicks . . . er . . . children you have, Lion," the counselors agreed. "What a fine, feathered family!"

"Uh-huh!" said Chief Counselor Fox. "Note the resemblance."

"Stop him," Mama and Papa Ostrich cried. "Everyone knows those are our children."

But no one dared stop Lion as he walked off with the chicks.

Mama and Papa Ostrich decided to call a meeting of all the animals. Though the counselors did nothing, Mama and Papa were sure Lion would have to listen if all the animals spoke up for them.

Mama Ostrich sought out Mongoose at once. He'd helped her before, and she knew he was clever.

"How could the counselors let Lion get away?" she asked Mongoose after telling him her story. "They promised to help me get my chicks back from Lion."

"Aha, you see," said Mongoose, "it's easy for them to stand up for your rights to your face. To stand up for your rights in Lion's face is another thing."

"Well," said Mama Ostrich, "Lion may be hard-hearted, but there is a proverb: 'Infinite boiling will soften the stone.'"

"Uh-huh," said Mongoose, "but another proverb says: 'In the court where the fox is the judge, the jury foxes and the witnesses foxes, the goose doesn't stand a chance.' And you're a bird among animals."

"Oh, my!" clacked Mama Ostrich. "What can I do? I won't give up till my children are home again."

"Listen," said Mongoose. "Before you call all the animals together, dig a tunnel under the tall ant hill at the meeting ground."

"A tunnel?" asked Mama Ostrich. "What for?"

"Don't ask, just dig it," said Mongoose. "Start digging the tunnel near the assembly place. Uh-huh, go to it and do it. Dig it large enough for me, but too small for Lion! Dig, dig, dig till you've dug through to the opposite side of the ant hill. Well, all right, dig, dig, dig! When it's all dug out, don't breathe a word about the tunnel to anyone. You dig? Leave the rest to me."

Mama Ostrich dug the tunnel clear through even though she didn't know what good it would do. Then she and Papa Ostrich called all the animals to the meeting.

The animals gathered at the meeting place by the tall anthill. Chief Counselor Fox and the counselors sat facing the assembly.

"Order, order!" commanded Chief Counselor Fox. He blew his horn, "Cheerooo-cheerooo!" to quiet the animals.

"We've a serious matter to settle today," he said. "Mama and Papa Ostrich claim Lion has taken their children. Lion claims they're his. To whom do you say they belong?"

The animals looked at the chicks trembling between Lion's paws. They looked at Mama and Papa Ostrich. Uh-huh, they were not fooled.

"Ready to vote?" asked Chief Counselor Fox.

Lion stood up on two feet.

"I'll take your votes, personally, one by one," he said in a menacing tone. "You don't mind if I do, do you, chief?"

Chief Counselor Fox knew this was against the rules, but he didn't dare deny Lion's request.

Lion approached the animals one by one and took the vote. He looked straight into their eyes and asked, "Whose?"

The animals quaked and were quick to see that chicks could be cubs. In turn each agreed that the chicks were indeed Lion's children, uh-huh, uh-huh!

By the time Lion reached Mongoose, all of the animals had gone back on their promise to support Mama and

Papa Ostrich. All the votes were in favor of Lion.

"Well, Mongoose," said Lion. "Let me have your vote. That will end this meeting. I'm hungry and I want to take my children home . . . to eat."

Mama and Papa Ostrich knew just what Lion meant. They stared in alarm at Mongoose.

Mongoose looked straight back at Lion. He spoke loud and clear for all to hear.

"Lion lies!" Mongoose exclaimed. "We all have eyes. Lion may stand on two feet now, but he looks absurd. He is no bird! You all know the proverb: 'A log may lie in the water for ten years, but it will never become a crocodile!' When has anyone ever heard that fur can beget feathers? Uh-uh! The chicks are Ostriches!"

Lion stood stock still. He was stunned for the moment. And that moment was all that Mongoose needed. He leaped for the tunnel and escaped down the hole.

Lion came to just in time to see Mongoose flee down the hole. Lion chased after him and dived for the hole. Pow! He fell back and rolled over. Lion roared in anger and tried again, but he was too large to fit through.

The meeting broke up, and the animals scattered. As they ran, they chanted:

"Fur beget feathers, fur beget feathers,
No one's ever seen fur beget feathers."

Mama and Papa Ostrich quickly untied their chicks and the eight Ostriches sprinted all the way home.

Lion pounced back and forth before the hole. He pawed and clawed at the entrance.

"Come out, come out!" he roared. "I'll give you 'fur beget feathers'!"

Mongoose didn't hear a word of Lion's fuss over fur and feathers. He had sped right out the other end of the tunnel and kept going.

"I know you're in there," Lion called. "You've got to come out this way, and I won't budge from here until you do. You sly Mongoose. Dog knows your name!"

Insults didn't bring Mongoose out either. He was now safe at home.

Lion finally tired of the roaring, pouncing and clawing. He crouched down on the ground before the hole and waited for Mongoose to come out.

Hours passed. Lion still sat there, too stubborn to move.

Lion grew hungrier and hungrier . . .

"I'll eat Mongoose when I catch him."

. . . and weaker and weaker . . .

"He won't give me the slip!"

. . . and fainter and thinner . . .

"Where's my Mongoose dinner?"

. . . till at last, hush, he wasted away.

Then Mama and Papa Ostrich stretched and strutted freely with their chicks.

Mama Ostrich said, "I've got a present of mangoes for Mongoose."

"Oh, mangoes for Mongoose! Mangoes for Mongoose," the six chicks cried.

Mama Ostrich and her chicks went to visit Mongoose to thank him. Mongoose came out to meet them.

The six chicks cheeped:

> *"Fur beget feathers, fur beget feathers,*
> *No one's ever seen fur beget feathers."*

They danced around Mongoose, singing their song, and Mama Ostrich handed Mongoose two large, juicy mangoes.

> *Clap for Ostrich, Mongoose, too.*
> *Stamp for Lion. Shoo! Shoo!*

The Son of the Wind

Mother Wind and her son lived in a round hut on a hill. The son of the wind had no playmates. He often sat alone and looked out of the window.

When the winds blew gently, the springbok grazed on the slopes of the nearby hills. When storm winds blew, the springbok sheltered in the lee of the distant hill.

The son of the wind would look out of his window when the wind was mild and watch the wandering springbok on the slopes. He whistled softly as he watched, sweetly and softly to soothe the longing of his secret wish.

One day, the son of the wind looked out and saw a boy coming up the hill. Whooree! He had whistled his secret wish so sweetly, it had sprung to life.

The son of the wind took up his ball. He blew open the door of the hut, whoosh! and rushed out to play.

"O Nakati!" he called. "There it goes!" And he rolled the ball to the boy.

Nakati was surprised to hear his name called by a stranger.

"Who is this?" he wondered as he caught the ball. "How is it that he knows my name? I do not know his."

"O friend," Nakati called. "There it goes!" And he rolled the ball back.

Nakati did not know that the stranger was the son of the wind. Wind blows everywhere, past huts and heights, through hollows. Wind whispers its wishes wherever it blows. A child somewhere, unawares, hears the wind's wish and follows.

Wherever wind goes, wind listens. What wind hears,

wind remembers. Wind carries our secrets. Wind knows our names.

"O Nakati! There it goes!" cried the son of the wind.

"O friend! There it goes!" cried Nakati.

They laughed and clapped as they rolled the ball between them. Back and forth the ball rolled to the calls of "O Nakati! There it goes! O friend! There it goes!" Up and down the slope the ball rolled till Mother Wind came out and called her son.

Nakati listened, hoping to hear his friend's name. He heard only sounds like the noise of the wind.

"O Nakati! When will you come to roll the ball with me again?"

"I will come again tomorrow and roll the ball with you then."

The son of the wind whistled his delight and waved good-bye to Nakati. He ran to his mother and held her hand as they walked up the hill. Then whoosh! They blew open the door of their hut and disappeared inside.

Nakati turned and ran toward home. He could hardly wait to ask his mother about the boy on the hill. She knew everyone who lived in these hills. He startled a springbok as he ran along, but he did not even notice.

"Mother! Mother!" he cried as he ran past his father into the hut. "Tell me my friend's name!"

Nakati's mother caught her son as he ran into her arms.

"First quiet down and catch your breath," she said. "Now tell me, what friend are you talking about?"

"The boy who lives on the hill," said Nakati. "He calls my name when he rolls the ball to me. He says, 'O Nakati! There it goes!' and I can only say, 'O friend! There it goes!' I would like to call his name when I roll the ball to him, just as he calls mine."

"I cannot tell you his name now, Nakati," his mother said. "You must wait until your father has finished building the windshelter for our hut. Then I will tell you his name."

Each day Nakati went to the hill and rolled the ball with his playmate. The son of the wind would call "O Nakati! There it goes!" as he rolled the ball, but Nakati could only reply, "O friend! There it goes!" as he rolled the ball in return.

Whenever Mother Wind called her son, Nakati listened to hear his name. He heard only wind sounds like "whooree" and "goowow."

"Why is it that every time I listen for my friend's name, I hear only the sound of the wind?" he wondered. Yet even though he listened carefully to Mother Wind's voice, the noise of the wind was all he heard.

Nakati helped his father so that the surrounding screen of bushes sheltering the hut would be finished faster.

"When the shelter is finished," his father said, "we will go and catch a springbok together. The air is calm and they still feed in our hills."

Finally there was little work left to do for the shelter.

"O Mother!" Nakati exclaimed. "Father's work is almost finished. Tell me now my friend's name!"

"I will tell you his name, Nakati," his mother said. "But first you must promise to keep it as a secret, you must keep it to yourself. When you roll the ball back and forth with the boy on the hill, do not say the name I will tell you until you see your father sitting down. Then you will know that the shelter is finished. Remember, do not say the name until then. You must keep it as a secret. You must keep it to yourself."

"I will wait," said Nakati. "I will keep the name a secret until I see Father sitting down. Now tell me his name."

"Your playmate is the son of the wind," said his mother. "When you say his name, it may startle him and cause him to fall. If he falls, the winds will begin to blow. So when you say his name, you must run home to the shelter of the hut as fast as you can, for he could blow you away."

"I will run, Mother. I will run faster than the wind. Tell me, please tell me! What is his name?"

"Listen carefully, my son," said his mother. "His name is Whooree-kuan-kuan. It is Gwow-gwowbootish. He is Whooree-kuan-kuan Gwow-gwowbootish."

Nakati tapped his forehead in surprise.

"Whooree-kuan-kuan Gwow-gwowbootish," he repeated. "Why, I've known it all along. I heard it everytime his mother called, but I thought it was just the sound of the wind blowing. So it was Mother Wind who called!"

Nakati snapped his fingers and spun round and round like a whirlwind.

"So that is the secret: The sound of the wind blowing is the son of the wind's name! Whooree-kuan-kuan Gwow-gwowbootish."

Now Nakati knew the secret of his friend's name. He ran off to play with him.

The son of the wind saw Nakati coming. Whoosh! He blew open the door and ran out with the ball.

"O Nakati! There it goes!" cried the son of the wind. He rolled the ball as Nakati ran up the hill.

Nakati caught the ball. He remembered his promise to his mother. He looked across the field to his hut. His father had just come out to finish work on the shelter.

"O friend! There it goes!" Nakati called as he rolled the ball back.

The ball rolled back and forth between the boys. Each time Nakati looked to his home, he saw his father at work on the shelter.

"O Nakati! There it goes!"

Nakati held the ball a moment and looked to his father.

He rolled the ball back, saying, "O friend! There it goes!"
for his father still had not finished work on the shelter.

Just as Nakati felt he could no longer hold the secret of
his friend's name, he saw his father sit down by the door
of the hut. At last his father had finished work on the
shelter.

Nakati caught the ball as it came to him. Then rolling it back to the son of the wind he called:

"O Whooree-kuan-kuan! There it goes! Gwow-gwowbootish! There it goes! Whooree-kuan-kuan Gwow-gwowbootish! There it goes!"

The son of the wind looked up in surprise to hear his name called by his friend. He began to rock back and forth on his feet. Nakati did not wait for the ball to reach his playmate. Remembering his mother's warning, he turned and ran.

The ball hit the son of the wind's knees and rolled forward. As he rocked and reached for the ball, he lost his balance and fell sprawling in a hollow of the ground. There he lay, pulling at the tall grass and kicking violently.

Nakati looked back as he ran and saw that his friend had fallen. As the son of the wind rolled and tossed on the ground, the winds began to stir.

Whooree-kuan-kuan Gwow-gwowbootish bent his knees, and a snapping sound shivered the air. The winds swirled. Whooree-kuan-kuan caught the winds and spun them into a great ball.

"O Nakati! There it goes!" he called, and he flung the wind-ball after his fleeing friend.

The wind-ball rolled down the hill and bounced after Nakati. Nakati knew he could not hold back the wind-ball,

he could not roll the wind-ball back to Whooree-kuan-kuan. He felt the ball of wind at his back, Gwow-gwowbootish!

Now Nakati really ran. He ran faster than the wind, Whooree-kuan-kuan Gwow-gwowbootish! He ran into his hut and slammed the door.

The ball of wind hurled itself against the door and twirled round and round the hut, but it could not get in.

Whooree-kuan-kuan Gwow-gwowbootish rolled about where he had fallen, enjoying the strength that came to him from lying down outdoors. As he rolled on his back, kicking his feet, the storm winds increased. He bent his knees, and noises rent the air.

The winds swept along, howling and uprooting bushes, overturning weak shelters, shaking huts. Dust filled the air.

Mother Wind heard the commotion and knew that her son had fallen. She blew open the door whoosh! and rushed out of the hut calling:

"Whooree-kuan-kuan Gwow-gwowbootish! Get up! Get up!"

The son of the wind lay swirling in the whirling dust. He shouted for joy, whooree! Whooree! He didn't hear his mother. He bent one knee, the winds screeched. He cracked both knees, the winds screamed.

Whooree-kuan-kuan's mother ran up to him. She grasped him firmly and set him on his feet.

While the son of the wind lay on the ground, strong winds had blown up a storm and caused the dust to rise. Now that the son of the wind stood on his feet, the winds died down and the dust settled.

That is why the Bushmen say that when the wind stands up, the wind is still, so still it seems to be lying down, asleep. It is then that the wind blows gently.

But when the wind lies down, it is then that it seems to be standing up, awake. It is then that the wind blows violently.

While the storm winds raged, Nakati and his parents were safe and sheltered within their hut.

Nakati's father said, "Our shelter is sturdy, still I wish the wind would soon blow gently for us. The strong winds have driven the springbok away. They have gone beyond the distant hill to drink of the river yonder that flows behind that hill. If the wind stands up and we go as quietly as the wind, we may slip down to the river and catch a springbok there, before the setting of the sun."

When all was still, Nakati stepped outdoors. He looked to the distant hill of which his father had spoken. The springbok would be there, behind that hill.

Then he looked up to the hill where he had rolled the ball with the son of the wind. He whispered the name to himself, "Whooree-kuan-kuan Gwow-gwowbootish.

"Ah," Nakati said. "Aha, I see. You may walk with the

wind, you may talk with the wind, you may run and play whatever games you wish with the wind. But when the wind calls your name, you must not call the wind's name. Keep this name secret.

"It is Whooree-kuan-kuan. It is Gwow-gwowbootish! Whooree-kuan-kuan Gwow-gwowbootish!"

Jackal's Favorite Game

Children, let me tell you 'bout Jackal and Hare.
Said, "Listen while I tell a tale of Jackal and Hare.
Jackal played at friendship,
Said, 'Playing's all I care'!"

Jackal played at friendship with Hare.

Jackal never cared at all how Hare felt, uh-uh! Jackal laughed his sad Jackal laugh and cared about nothing but playing games. He had the bad habit of tackling and tickling Hare to force him to play. So whenever Jackal saw Hare coming, Jackal put him down. Uh-huh, Jackal tackled Hare to the ground.

"La-boohoo-laha," laughed Jackal. "Playing's all I care!"

"Let go!" gasped Hare as Jackal tackled him to the prickly grass.

Jackal didn't listen to Hare's cry, uh-uh! Jackal didn't care. He only played at friendship, said "Playing's all I care." Then Jackal tickled Hare as he rolled him in the prickly grass.

"Let me hee-haw up!" giggled Hare as Jackal tickled. "Stop tickling me, hee-hee!"

"La-boohoo-laha!" laughed Jackal. "La-boohoo-laha!"

Every time they met, to get the games started, Jackal tackled and tickled Hare. He never let Hare up until he agreed to play hide-and-seek. That was Jackal's favorite game and he always cried out, "Me first! Me first! You're it!"

One day Hare was out, playing all by himself. He was having a good time too, doing the Hare-Hop and singing:

"I jump high, jump higher,
Get ready, jump steady,
To the sky, yeah!"

"La-boohoo-laha, la-boohoo-laha."

"Uh-huh," said Hare. "That's Jackal's laugh. I'd better hide from that tickle-tackler."

Hare ducked behind a tree.

"Come out, come out, wherever you are!" cried Jackal. "I saw you jumping."

Hare didn't budge. He hummed to himself:

"Some friends are true friends,
Some are makes-you-blue friends,
You can tell by what they do
Who is true, who makes you blue.
And Jackal makes me blue."

"La-boohoo-laha, I know you're hiding," said Jackal. "Hide-and-seek is my favorite game and playing's all I care."

"Uh-huh!" said Hare. "I won't play if you tackle and tickle me."

"I won't tickle or tackle," said Jackal, "but you know hide-and-seek is my game. Me first! Me first!"

Hare stepped out of hiding and asked, "How come you always go first?"

Jackal clapped his paws, clicked his claws, snapped his jaws and said:

"Because I'm bigger than you,
Because I'm faster, too.
Because I'm tough as can be,
So don't you 'How come' me!"

Jackal's reasons didn't seem fair at all to Hare, but he didn't dare go on about it, uh-uh! Jackal went first.

Jackal spun Hare around three times.

"Now, lean against the tree and count out loud," Jackal said. "Close your eyes. No peeking!"

Hare closed his eyes and chanted:

"*Cabbages, peppers, carrots and peas,*
Count them by ones, by twos, by threes.
I'll find you first, then I'll plant these,
Cabbages, peppers, carrots and peas."

While Hare counted, Jackal skipped off and hid in a clump of bushes. He crouched low and covered himself with twigs and leaves. Jackal was sure that Hare would never find him in his bush disguise. He didn't notice that his tail stuck out. It switched back and forth as he sang:

"I cover myself with leaves.
I close my eyes.
You'll never, ever find me
Till I yell, 'Surprise!'"

Hare looked here. Hare looked there. So far, no Jackal anywhere. Hare put his hands on his hips and hopped to the bushes. He was about to hop on when he saw a tail switch.

"Uh-huh!" said Hare. "I never saw a tail-wagging bush before."

Hare walked up to the bush and called, "Come out! Come out, wherever you are. A telltale tail's told me you're in there."

Jackal didn't budge, but his tail switched on.

Hare called again, "Come out, come out wherever you are. I spy Jackal!"

Hare stamped on Jackal's tail.

"Yow!" yelled Jackal. He jumped up and the leaves and twigs fell off of him.

"Surprise! You thought I was a bush, eh! You didn't
see me. I go again."

"Uh-uh!" said Hare. "I go now. I knew you were there.
Your tail may be bushy, but bushes don't wag tails."

Jackal brushed that off.

"I said, 'I go again!'" Jackal insisted. "Remember:

> *I'm bigger than you.*
> *I'm faster, too.*
> *I'm tough as can be,*
> *So don't you 'I go' me!"*

Jackal reached out, snatched Hare and spun him around three times.

"Now, count, and don't say you won't," Jackal ordered.

"Not fair," Hare murmured to himself. He didn't like being cheated out of his turn. He closed his eyes and chanted softly, so softly he could hardly be heard:

> *"Cabbages, peppers, carrots, peas.*
> *Count by ones, by twos, by threes.*
> *I'll find you, then I'll plant these:*
> *Cabbages, peppers, carrots and peas."*

Jackal scampered off to a grove of trees. He broke off some branches, then he took a vine and tied the branches around his waist.

"La-boohoo-laha," laughed Jackal. "Hiding's the best part of hide-and-seek. Now, I'm a tree. If I close my eyes, Hare won't see me."

Jackal stood up straight and still. He tucked his tail in this time, then he closed his eyes.

Hare opened his eyes. He didn't see Jackal by the home base.

"Ready or not, here I come!" Hare called.

First Hare hopped to the bush where Jackal had crouched before. He beat about the bush. No Jackal there. Hare searched the high grasses and looked behind some stones. No traces of Jackal in either of those places.

Hare ran to the grove of trees. He saw a strange sight. A tree with two legs.

"Uh-huh," said Hare:

> *"Your eyes are closed,*
> *But I can see.*
> *I spy Jackal,*
> *One, two, three!"*

Hare poked Jackal in the ribs, jaa!

"Ow!" Jackal cried. He dropped his arms and the branches. "My eyes were closed. I looked like a tree. I didn't see you. How did you see me?"

"I kept my eyes open," said Hare. "You close yours now. It's my turn. You're it."

Jackal had taken two turns and he was tempted to take three, but he relented and let Hare take a turn, too.

Now it was Hare's turn to spin Jackal around three times and to tell him, "Count out loud, I want to hear you! And close your eyes. No peeking!"

Jackal closed his eyes and leaned against a tree. He'd rather hide than seek any day. But he'd find Hare and then he'd go again, uh-huh! His count was a blues chant:

> *Okra, cassava, coconuts and corn.*
> *Said, okra, cassava, coconuts, corn.*
> *I'll count them till I find you*
> *If it takes me all day long."*

As soon as Jackal began his chant, Hare hopped off to find a good hiding place. Bippity-bop-bop, he hopped, bippity-bop-bop. He looked back to see if Jackal was peeking. Paa-lam! Hare tripped over a tree root and fell into a hole. The hole was deep enough to keep Hare well hidden from sight.

"Eh, eh!" said Hare. "What luck! I couldn't have chosen a better hiding place."

Hare made himself at home in the hole. He leaned back and stared up at the tree branches and the sky. He enjoyed watching the butterflies and birds that flew by while he waited.

Jackal finished his hide-and-seek count and set out to find Hare. He poked about in a clump of bushes and called, "Come out, come out wherever you are!"

Hare heard the loud call from wherever Jackal looked. He didn't plan to come out of his hiding hole.

Jackal came closer. Hare didn't move or make a sound. He opened his eyes wide and looked up.

Jackal saw the holes by the tree roots and he began to look into them.

Hare heard Jackal's steps coming closer and closer. He knew he would soon be discovered, but Hare was a good hide-and-seek player. He wouldn't give up until he'd been caught.

"I see you. I see you!" Jackal cried each time he looked into a dark hole. But he hadn't seen Hare yet.

> *"You may have seen a spider,*
> *You may have seen a bee,*
> *You may have seen a cricket,*
> *But you haven't seen me."*

Just then Jackal came to the hole in which Hare was hiding. Jackal looked straight into two large eyes that stared up at him out of the dark. Hare knew he'd been caught.

"Aie yaie! Aie yaie!" yelled Jackal.

He tumbled over backwards and almost caught his foot in a hole. He got to his feet and fled.

"Eh, eh!" said Hare. "What is this? Jackal found me, yet he's running away. That's no way to play hide-and-seek."

"Aie yaie! Aie yaie!" Jackal cried as he ran. "I have seen the Big-Eyed Monster. The Big-Eyed Monster is after me!"

Hare hopped out of his hole and heard Jackal's cry.

"So that's why he fled. He thinks I'm a big-eyed monster."

Hare laughed and took off after Jackal, bippity-bop-bop, bippity-bop-hop.

"Here comes the Big-Eyed Monster," Hare called. "Here comes Hare, the Big-Eyed Monster!"

"Aie yaie! Aie yaie!" Jackal wailed. "Only a monster has eyes like that! Its head must be huge. It's body, big and brutal, I bet!"

Jackal was so frightened that he didn't look where he was running. His feet caught in a vine and tripped him up. Down he went, flam!

Jackal lay there crying and panting and kicking. He couldn't untangle the vine from his feet. He closed his eyes in fright.

"The Big-Eyed Monster will get me," he cried. "La-boohoo, la-boohoo."

Hare caught up with Jackal and loosened the vine from around his feet. Jackal kept his eyes shut.

"O Big-Eyed Monster," he cried. "La-boohoo, la-boohoo! I'll do whatever you ask. Don't eat me!"

Hare sang:

> *"Because I'm bigger than you,*
> *Because I'm faster, too,*
> *Because I'm tough as can be,*
> *So don't you 'Don't eat me!'"*

Jackal opened his eyes.

"La-boohoo-lala, Brother Hare!!" Jackal cried, "Save me! This hide-and-seek game is for real. The Big-Eyed Monster is after me."

"Don't be silly," said Hare. "Look at me!"

Hare shaded his face and opened his eyes wide.

"You, Brother Hare!" Jackal exclaimed. "You're the Big-Eyed Monster!"

"Uh-huh," said Hare. "You found me, but then you ran away bawling. That's no way to play hide-and-seek."

"You scared me," said Jackal. "You shouldn't hide in dark holes and open your eyes so big and wide, not when we play hide-and-seek. Uh-uh! That's my favorite game. Promise not to do it anymore."

"You said you'd do whatever I ask when I loosened the vine from your feet," said Hare. "Promise not to tackle and tickle me anymore."

Jackal and Hare exchanged promises right then and there, and they kept them. Uh-huh, they did. Jackal stopped playing friendship with Hare and became a true friend.

After that, when Jackal and Hare played games, Jackal often said: "You first, Brother Hare. You first."

Now that's true friendship, isn't it? Uh-huh!
And playing's all I care!

THE FOOLISH BOY

There was once a bean farmer and he had a good wife. They lived together in a thatched-roof hut. They hoped for children, but as yet they had none. Still, they had each other and that made them happy.

On farming days, they rose early and after breakfast they walked over the hill to work in their bean field.

"Hot beans and butter!" sang the farmer as he dug into the earth.

"Come for your supper!" sang his wife as she hoed a row beside him.

They sang as they worked because farming the land was their life and they enjoyed life. Towards sunset, they returned to their hut. For supper they ate hot beans and butter with the vegetables they grew in the little garden around their hut. They didn't have meat to eat but they didn't complain. For more than meat, they longed for a child.

The years passed and their prayers for a child went unanswered. God seemed not to hear.

One day the wife thought, "Perhaps our prayers get caught up in the thatch on the roof of the hut and never get higher. Tonight I'll pray outdoors."

That night, after her husband fell asleep, the wife got up quietly. She went outdoors and prayed, "Dear God, please send me a child, even if it be a foolish one."

Well all right! God heard that prayer. He sent her a son, a simpleton.

The farmer and his wife were overjoyed to have a child. They loved their son and named him Jumoke.

The mother carried her son on her back wherever she

went until Jumoke learned to walk. Then he followed behind his parents at work in the beanfield. One day as they
planted a row of bean seeds in the earth, Jumoke picked
up the seeds and put them in his little calabash.

A villager was passing by and called out to the parents,
"See what your foolish boy is doing?"

The parents turned and saw Jumoke with his calabash full of the beans they had just planted.

They didn't get excited.
They didn't get upset.
They didn't howl or holler
And they didn't throw a fit.

Instead, they taught him how to plant the seeds. But the name Foolish Boy stuck.

Years passed, and as the boy grew, so did the stories of his foolish ways. Finally everyone in the village called him Foolish Boy.

But his parents called him by his proper name and said, "His foolishness will make him wise. He'll surprise you one day."

Jumoke's mother was well known in the village for the delicious bean pies she baked. On big market days, she balanced a tray of bean pies on her head and set out for the market. Little Jumoke followed behind with a tray of mud pies on his head.

When they arrived in the marketplace, Jumoke set his tray of mud pies down beside his mother's tray of bean pies. The villagers bought his mother's pies quickly. She hardly had to cry out.

Jumoke cried out to all who came near or passed by, "Buy my dry mud pies!"

The villagers laughed.

"What a foolish boy Foolish Boy is!" they said to his mother.

She didn't get excited.
She didn't get upset.
She didn't howl or holler
And she didn't throw a fit.

Instead, she hugged him and said, "Don't all children say and do foolish things?"

Jumoke grew to be a fine youth. He no longer tried to sell mud pies in the market. He helped his mother carry her tray of bean pies. He'd learned many things, but the villagers still called him Foolish Boy.

One day Jumoke's parents left him to take care of the hut while they went to work in the bean field.

"Jumoke," his mother said, "cook a bean dinner for us to eat tonight."

That afternoon Jumoke put a pot filled with water on the fire. When the water boiled, he dropped in a bean and stirred.

"Don't stick to the bottom!" he said as he whipped up the bean. "Swim on top!"

When his parents returned from work, they asked:

"Is the bean dinner cooked?"

"It's in the pot," said Jumoke.

They looked in the pot. Jumoke's father shook his head and said, "A man must resign himself to what God has given him." His mother sighed.

But they didn't get excited.
They didn't get upset.
They didn't howl or holler
And they didn't throw a fit.

Instead his mother taught Jumoke how to cook a bean dinner. Then she taught her son different ways of preparing beans and how to make bean pies. She knew that although Jumoke did foolish things, he learned from his foolish ways.

One day Spider Ananse was out walking when he smelled beans cooking.

"Mmm-yum, beans," Spider said. "Smells good all right! Reminds me that my wife is cooking beans for supper tonight. Wish I had some meat to eat with those beans."

Spider followed his nose to Jumoke's hut. He saw several gazelles nibbling the vegetables in the garden around the hut.

"Oh neat! Meat!" Spider cried. "If only I had my traps with me!"

Just then Jumoke jumped out of the door and chased after the gazelles. He tried to catch one, but they all escaped.

"Hello, Foolish Boy," said Spider Ananse. "Do the gazelles often get into your vegetable garden?"

"No," said Jumoke. "They found our garden yesterday and they've come back today. I chase them, but I haven't caught one yet."

"Well, Foolish Boy," said Spider, "how would you like to eat gazelle meat with your beans tonight?"

Jumoke stamped his feet and clapped his hands.

"Well," said Spider Ananse, "I'll bring my traps, and we'll catch them. Cook up a large pot of beans for bait. I'll be right back."

Now Spider Ananse loved to play tricks on everyone. He was so quick and clever that no one managed to trick him.

Spider Ananse had never bothered to trick Foolish Boy. He had even told his wife that Foolish Boy would be so easy to trick it wouldn't be fun. But for good gazelle meat, Spider was ready to trick anyone.

"Foolish Boy will get to see good gazelle meat all right," said Spider, laughing as he ran home. "But he won't get to eat good gazelle meat tonight. I'll beat him out of his share of the treat. Too bad Foolish Boy is going to be so easy to cheat."

Spider soon returned, riding his donkey. He sat on a large, leather bag. The traps were strapped on the donkey's back.

As soon as the beans were cooked, Jumoke helped Spider set the traps with the bean-bait. Then they hid in the hut and waited.

Soon some gazelles smelled the beans and returned to the hut. They passed up the vegetables for the bean-bait and suddenly, wham! WHAM! the traps snapped shut. Two gazelles were caught and killed. The others fled.

Spider and Jumoke ran out of hiding. They opened the traps. Jumoke watched as Spider skinned the two gazelles.

"Bring out two large baskets, Foolish Boy," Spider said. "We'll separate the good meat, swell! from the poor meat, thud!"

Jumoke brought the baskets and set them down beside Spider.

"The good meat, swell! goes into the basket on the right," said Spider. "The poor meat, thud! goes into the basket on the left."

Spider Ananse cut up the meat. Jumoke placed the meat in the baskets and sang:

"Good meat, swell! basket on the right
Poor meat, thud! basket on the left."

All the while that Spider cut the meat, he kept an eye on Jumoke to be sure he didn't mix up the baskets. At last the cutting and the separation was done.

"Tell me now, Foolish Boy," Spider asked, "whose traps caught the gazelles?"

"Yours, Spider," Jumoke answered. "Now tell me, Spider, whose bean-bait caught the gazelles?"

"Don't be foolish, Foolish Boy!" said Spider. "What're your beans worth beside my traps? The good meat, swell! is my share. The poor meat, thud! is your share."

"Thud!" cried Jumoke. "Thud! That's no fair share!"

But Spider didn't care about being fair when he could get away with such a slick trick.

"Go and drive my donkey here, Foolish Boy, while I empty the good meat, swell! into my bag. And be quick about it!"

Jumoke brooded on Spider's mean trick as he went in

search of the donkey. He mumbled and grumbled till he found the donkey. Suddenly Jumoke smiled. He had an idea. He drove the donkey deep into the bush and returned empty-handed.

"Where is my donkey, Foolish Boy?" Spider demanded.

"She ran off into the bush before I could catch her," Jumoke answered.

"Fool, you fool Foolish Boy!" cried Spider. "You let my donkey get away. Here, finish filling my bag with the good meat, swell! I will go and get the donkey myself. She will come if I call."

Jumoke waited until Spider was well out of sight. Then quickly he took Spider's bag of good meat, swell! and emptied it into the corn bin in the hut.

Then Jumoke tipped the poor meat, thud! into Spider's bag. He put two good pieces of meat, swell! at the top of the bag and tied it up.

Spider Ananse's donkey had circled back when Spider called. She stood at the side of the hut and watched as Jumoke filled Spider's bag with the bones and scraps. Spider caught up with his donkey just as Jumoke finished tying up the bag.

"You see, Foolish Boy, I told you she'd come if I called," Spider said. "Have you finished packing my bag?"

"Oh, yes," said Jumoke. "And it's heavy. Here, let me help you lift it onto your donkey."

Jumoke steadied the heavy bag and the traps while Spider strapped them on the donkey's back.

Spider laughed as he headed for home, thinking he would have one big surprise for his wife that night.

"Enjoy your dinner, Foolish Boy!" Spider sang as he drove the donkey along:

"Good meat, swell! Poor meat, thud!
Fooling folk is in my blood.
To fool a fool may not be fair,
But I should worry, I should care!"

Spider beat out the rhythms on the poor donkey's back. A-whack! A-whack! A-whack!

"Faster! Faster!" Spider cried. "I'm getting hungry!"

The blows stung and finally the donkey could take it no longer. She sang out:

"Swell or thud; like it or not,
It's stomach, liver and scraps you've got."

"What are you saying?" cried Spider.

He gave the donkey a harder whack with his stick. "Sing rather:

"Even Dog and Cat will have a treat,
For I took the tip-top tasty meat."

But no matter how hard Spider hit, the donkey continued to sing:

"Cat and Dog will have a treat,
They'll get the tip-top tasty meat.
But swell or thud, like it or not,
It's stomach, liver and scraps you've got."

Spider was so aggravated by these words that he beat the donkey all the way home.

When Jumoke's parents returned from work in their bean field, they entered the hut and smelled the meaty aroma coming from the hot beans pot.

"Hot beans and butter," sang Jumoke as they looked in the pot.

"And meat for our supper!" his mother exclaimed.

"Couldn't be better," his father said.

"There's meat for days to come, too," said Jumoke. He led his parents to the corn bin.

"Where did you get all this good meat?" his parents asked.

Jumoke danced and sang:

"You didn't get excited.
You didn't get upset.
You didn't howl or holler
And you didn't throw a fit.

And now I've done something good."

Then Jumoke told his parents the story of how Spider Ananse had tried to trick him, and how he had turned the trick on Spider.

"Why, good meat, swell! Poor meat, thud!" sang the parents. "You sure tricked that trickster Spider. No one has ever done that before."

"No more talk now," said Jumoke, laughing. "Come for your supper."

But first his mother and father hugged him tight. Then they all sat down to a delicious supper of hot beans and butter and good meat, swell!

Spider Ananse reached home and called his wife:

"Koki! Hey, Koki! I've a surprise for you. Bring the large calabash that belonged to your ancestors. This is a special occasion."

Cat and Dog heard Spider and came running. Cat rubbed up against Spider's legs! Dog sat up and begged.

Spider opened the sack. He tossed one top piece of meat to Cat. He tossed another top piece of meat to Dog.

Spider's wife returned with the large calabash. She saw Cat and Dog running off with juicy morsels of meat in their mouths.

"Aha!" said Spider Ananse, laughing. "See that, eh? Tonight Dog and Cat eat good meat, swell! And so will we, Koki. So will we! Just wait till you see!"

Koki set the large calabash on the ground, and Spider poured the contents of the bag into it.

"What is this?" cried Koki. "Bones! Stomach! Scraps! Is
this what you want my good calabash for—the calabash of
my ancestors?"

"Oh, no! Oh, no!" cried Spider. "Poor meat, thud! How
did that happen? Here, Cat! Here, Dog!"

But Cat and Dog had run off with the good meat, swell!
And would not come back.

Koki picked up a leg bone, shook it at Spider and
shouted, "You give Dog and Cat good meat, swell! And
this is what you give me? Well, this is what I give you!"

Koki swung the leg bone, wham! and gave Spider one
hard blow across his back.

The donkey sang:

"Swell or thud, like it or not.
It's stomach, liver and scraps you've got."

"Oh, donkey," Spider wailed, "you were telling the truth after all and I beat you. If only I had listened to you instead."

Spider stroked the donkey gently and said, "How I have wronged you! I promise never to beat you again. I, the **trickster, deserve** blows for letting a fool fool me. Not you! What a wicked trick he played on me!"

"You don't mean you let Foolish Boy trick you?" said Koki in surprise. "But you've always said it wasn't worth tricking Foolish Boy, it would be too easy."

"Oh, I know! Oh, oh, oh!" wailed Spider.

"A simple switch-trick like that, and you fell for it, Spider!" said Koki.

Koki was about to serve Spider another well-deserved leg bone blow, when suddenly her anger gave way. She dropped the leg bone, threw her arms around the donkey's neck and burst out laughing.

The donkey hee-hawed along with her.

"Thud!" said Spider. "Just wait till tomorrow. I'll get even with him!"

The next morning Spider Ananse set out to call on Jumoke. He was determined to even the score before the story of Foolish Boy's switch-trick made the rounds in the village.

Jumoke's parents had prepared him for Spider's return before they left for work in the fields.

When Spider arrived, there sat Jumoke at the entrance to his hut, covered from head to foot with ashes.

Spider knew this was a sign of sorrow. He couldn't imagine why Foolish Boy was in mourning, and he didn't care about it either. He had troubles enough of his own.

"Peace be upon you," said Spider Ananse.

"And upon you, peace," Jumoke replied.

Spider didn't waste a minute. He burst out crying, "You cheated me, Foolish Boy! You played a trick on me. I opened my bag of meat at home and found only poor meat, thud!"

"Oh, Spider," Jumoke cried, "don't talk to me about good meat, swell! and poor meat, thud! It's all bad meat to me now."

"How can that be? You took all the good meat, swell!" said Spider.

"Yes," said Jumoke, "but those gazelles that were caught in your traps were the Chief's gazelles. He's sent a messenger to my father. He wants to know what happened to the gazelles you caught."

"I'm not in this!" said Spider.

"The Chief wants the gazelles back, Spider, because they belong to him."

"Oh, poor Foolish Boy," said Spider. "I see you are in trouble."

"Help me, Spider," Jumoke pleaded. "Take the good meat, swell! before the Chief finds it here."

"I wouldn't touch it, Foolish Boy," said Spider. "I must go home now. Koki, my wife, is waiting for me."

Spider bent down and sprinkled more ashes on Jumoke.

"I'm sorry, but that's all I can do to help you, Foolish Boy," said Spider. "May God make it easy for you. Good-bye!"

Spider Ananse couldn't get away from there fast enough. He ran home chuckling to himself.

"Aha, aha! Foolish Boy is indeed in trouble. I was afraid for a moment that I couldn't get free of him. What a clever trickster I am!

"This is just the way I intended it to turn out!"

"Good meat, swell! Poor meat, thud!
Fooling folk is in my blood.
To fool a fool may not be fair,
But I should worry, I should care!"

But you and I know better. The villagers knew better.
Even the donkey knew better.

When Spider Ananse learned that Foolish Boy had
tricked him not just once, but twice, he took to his bed.
He lay there for ten days and wouldn't touch meat. Then
he got up, packed his goods and moved away from that
village.

From the stories we've heard since then of Spider
Ananse, we know that he's still busy tricking others. But
ever since Foolish Boy tricked him, he's moved on whenever he's been tricked. And since that does happen sometimes, stories of Spider Ananse have spread far and wide.

Jumoke's parents loved him and had been patient with
him. They had taught him to learn from his mistakes.
They believed that in this way even a simpleton could become wise.

The villagers now praised the boy's wit more than they had ever laughed at his foolishness. They no longer called him Foolish Boy. They called him by his proper name, Jumoke, just as his parents always had.

And more than ever before, everyone loved the child.

Poor meat, thud! Good meat, swell!
Don't you know another story to tell?